THE WIFE

It was as if at some point in his adolescence he had stopped thinking 'I' and started thinking 'We'. Life before that had been a struggle between his parents and himself. Now he conceived of a much more general 'them' against a self-contained new entity called 'us'. Accordingly, he looked around him to find a girl on whom he could impose the splendid vision of this unity. She must be a partner in his own image, a mirror reflection of himself and all his dreams. There would be no mystery about her, for what did one need to learn about so familiar a person as one's twin? He would tell her who she was. And when she had been told, they would become a pair, invincible against the world as long as they walked hand in hand through the forest, or slept side by side with the sword between them, or sat throne by throne like the kings and queens of fairy tales.

THE WIFE

Judith Burnley

ARROW BOOKS

A Sparrow Book
Published by Arrow Books Limited
17–21 Conway Street, London W1P 6JD

An imprint of the Hutchinson Publishing Group

London Melbourne Sydney Auckland
Johannesburg and agencies throughout the world

First published by William Heinemann 1977
First published in paperback by Pan Books 1978
Arrow edition 1983

© Judith Burnley 1977

Made and printed in Great Britain
by The Anchor Press Ltd,
Tiptree, Essex

ISBN 0 09 932370 2

For F. B.
with love

"You cannot be in two places at once, except you're a bird."

Irish politician
in the Dáil.

Part One

1

Early morning in a third floor flat in a London square. Grey light. Muffled sounds. She sits at her dressing table half asleep, drinking coffee, painting her eyes. He finishes his coffee. He is always first. He folds the newspaper, puts on his shoes and tells her he's ready. He is always ready.

"I'm off," he says, and drops a kiss from considerable height on her unbrushed hair. He shuts the door. "Don't be late home," he calls, threatening her. He shuts the outer door. The lift hums. The old house vibrates as the street door bangs. She hears without hearing the revving engine of an expensive sports car, sees without seeing the car slide round the corner of the square and into the race.

She goes to the window and lets more grey light into the room. She swims up slowly into the morning from a great depth. She finishes her toilet, packs a large bag carefully with pots and packages from the kitchen, books and papers from the living room, letters, cheques and make-up from the dressing table. Fifteen minutes after him she repeats his pattern. The door clicks. The lift hums. The house vibrates. She says good morning to the porter. She walks to the corner of the square and hails a taxi.

She stops the taxi in another square in another part of central London. She pays the cabbie, goes up some steps, says good morning to the porter and takes the lift to the third floor. She opens a door with a key and shuts it quietly. She goes into the kitchen and puts on the kettle. She puts her bag down, takes out the pots and packages and puts them in fridge and cupboard. She lays a tray, makes a pot of tea and two slices of toast and marmalade. She takes her coat off. She balances the tray and quietly opens an adjoining door. She enters the darkness, puts the tray by the bed, crosses the room and opens the curtains. She sits on the bed and watches the man asleep there as he wakes. He groans and stretches. He says, "Goo' morning, darling." She kisses him. She pours two cups of tea. He struggles upright and she props the pillows and gives him his cup. He kisses the hand round the cup. Grey light. Tea-drinking sounds.

"How late did you work?"
"Late."
"How did it go?"
He shrugs.

He tells her a dream he had in which they both figured. It was vivid and hideous, like Breughel, like Bacon. She says:

"I wish you'd dream Chagall. At least *I* could sleep peacefully at night."

They drank from blue cups, among blue sheets in a blue room, and the grey light fell softly on their skin.

We aim for Bonnard, she thought. *But there are always our dreams*.

She takes the tray, goes into the kitchen, washes the cups. She dries her hands, puts on her coat, takes her bag. He's washing his face in the bathroom, head forward, water splashing. She kisses the back of his neck. "I'll see you this evening," she says.

She goes down into the street. The branches of trees have changed colour with the increasing light. She walks down two eighteenth century streets, under an ornamental clock and round a corner into a steel and plate glass building. Newspaper House.

"Good morning, Miss Cornish," says the commissionaire. She takes the lift to the third floor.

"Good morning, Mrs Cornish," says the receptionist.

The Features Editor, Miles Prendergast, a weedy jester in the last days of his youth is waiting for her in her office. He never uses his own. He helps her off with her coat and presses his knuckles fiercely into her armpits.

"Are your armpits sexy?" he asks.

She twists away from him and sits down behind her desk. He sits on her chair facing her like a plaintiff while she sorts through a sheaf of interviews. She knows without looking how his body droops, bony, like uncooked spaghetti, over the chair.

"I could make them sexy," he says.

Oh God!

"I *know* you could," she allows.

In less than a second he's collected his limbs and is sitting tall. He says "When? When will you let me?" so fast that the leer comes up behind it. Question and leer remain unanswered. As always.

A girl comes in with a bulky file marked MARRIAGE TODAY SERIES. She puts it on Sarah's desk.

"He was on to me this morning," said Miles gloomily. "He" was the editor of the newspaper they worked for.

"He must have had a bad night. 'What d'you want to do a series on marriage for?' he asked me. 'I thought it was dying.' That's why we're doing it, I told him."

"Quick as a flash," said Sarah, scribbling busily.

"Yeah, quick as a flash," said Miles.

"So it's '*The Death of Marriage*' now, is it? Or do you prefer '*Is Marriage Dead*'?"

"Haven't we even got the title yet? What happened to '*Is there a Life After Marriage*'?"

"It's been used," said Sarah. "But don't despair. I've got some kinky ones here. '*Married Bondage*'," she reads, "or '*Tied, Gagged, and Married*'. Very fashionable. All whips and flag."

"'*Hanged, Drawn and Married*,'" says Miles, slightly mollified, as always, by his own poor jokes. "*Married Alive*." He's aiming darts at a chart from the other side of the room.

"Judging by the stuff I've got from the wives so far," Sarah tells him, "it certainly won't be '*Happily Ever After*'."

"Women," says Miles. "Always grumbling."

"You don't like women, do you, Miles?"

"I do better than that. I fuck 'em," says Miles.

Two young women talk together in the marble spaces of the Tate Gallery. Tall Mel, elegantly carrying her tender face forward on her long neck, turning it this way and that, a giraffe looking for leaves from the top of the tree. Sarah, small, narrow, dark and compact, drawing sights and sounds towards her, absorbing, secreting. She'll digest or discard her impressions later, privately, in her lair. They continue the conversation they've been having since they first met years ago.

They move among objects of great weight and beauty: huge curving figures of polished bronze with stomachs hollow yet emphatically pregnant; womb-like shapes in wood the colour of conkers. They pause for a moment by an ovoid sculpted in marble so clear the veins and membranes show beneath the skin.

"I daren't touch it," says Sarah. "I'm sure it's somebody's last chance. Don't you feel your private parts are scattered round this room?"

"And me with the curse," says Mel.

They wander on, discussing the details of their menstrual cycles. "Every month we have a wake, Bill and I," says Mel. At pre-menstrual tension they stop because Sarah grabs Mel's arm and points: "That huge reclining back over there. See if you can guess from here what sex it is and what it represents. I'm guessing too. I haven't seen the front either."

Mel stares. "Oh God," she says. "Trust you. Of course. That solid, sheltering back. What else?"

Together they walk around it till they're staring at the front. Triumph. Triumph and pain. It's mother and child. Or mother and child again.

Down the stairs they go to the Whistler room. Coffee and salads, limericks and gloom. Mel goes to get more coffees. Sarah takes a paper napkin. Scribbles.

In the room the women come and go
Talking of Michelangelo.
In awe at Moore, the women came and went.
Childless among pregnant bronze.
Let us lament.

"I feel like an empty room," says Mel. She writes:

A childless woman is an empty room
Take that inscription for my marble tomb.

They laugh at one another easily. No bitterness. Not yet. "Womb, room, tomb," says Sarah. "You're in a bad way, my girl. You ought to see a doctor."

Outside the gallery they part and Sarah takes a taxi to an interview.

She pays off the taxi somewhere in Battersea and climbs the dark stairway of a mansion block. A door is opened to her by a pale girl of about twenty-five with wild darting eyes and arms thin as wrists. She follows the girl down a corridor strewn with toys to a dark living room where they sit on the only two unbroken chairs. The girl lights a cigarette, puffs nervously, offers Sarah tea, which she declines.

"The kids are only out of the way for half an hour," says the girl. "What do you want to know?" When the girl gets going she talks faster than Sarah can scrawl. She gets most of it down and goes back to her office to type it out.

He'd come home and find me lying on the
floor crying and the place in chaos, and
the baby crawling all over the place,
crying too. He was frightfully cross
with me. You can't blame him. He used to
shake me and shake me and pour iron
stuff down me. I had an iron deficiency,
you see, after the first one. I'd lost a
lot of blood. And then, just when I'd
healed up a bit, I got pregnant again.
I think he did it on purpose. He thought
I'd built up such a block about sex and
about babies I'd never have another one
if I didn't have it then. I was terribly
tired all the time and I just couldn't
cope. I suppose I wanted him to show
sympathy and to make a fuss of me. But
it just angered him that I couldn't
cope, and I was always tired or ill or
miserable. I didn't want anything to do
with sex. You can't blame him for
wanting someone else, can you? I mean
she was just a girl he met on a blind
date. He would never leave me and the
children. I know that. And when she
wrote those letters to me when I was in
hospital having the baby—I think that
really put him off her. I mean she
didn't have to write and tell me everything they did together and what he did
to her in bed. I was very upset and I
was ill and everything after the baby
and I was really at the bottom. You
know. For quite a while. But then I
seemed to come to a conclusion. You
know: I'd survived. I think I was
surprised to discover that: that I'd
survived. And I think I realised then he
wasn't sensitive to me as a person, and

wouldn't ever be, and it wasn't like
that. I was a separate person. I could
be an independent person with all sorts
of areas and interests that were nothing
to do with him.

She files the interview in a folder marked MARRIAGE
TODAY: *Interviews with Wives*, in a section of the filing
system marked RESEARCH. On her desk is a pile of post, a
message from her secretary saying "Please 'phone dentist,
and your mother;" a message from the telephonist: "Mrs
Cornish, your grocer called. He hasn't got any Greek
olive oil. He is sending you French instead." A pile of
new books about the breakdown of class/morals/religion/
marriage/working-class sexuality in Great Britain. A
lavish book on Erotic Art and a rude note with a ruder
drawing from Miles.

She collects names and details of her interviews for
tomorrow, checks the addresses, and leaves the office.

She walks round the corner, under the ornamental
clock and down two eighteenth century streets. She lets
herself in with her key. An elegant masculine figure is
reclining, shoes off, on the sofa, watching the television
news. She kisses his head, flops into a chair, blinks
absently at the screen.

He says, "Tell me about your day."

She says, "Not with that noise in competition."

He says, "Come and lie down."

She complies. They kiss and make noises of kissing and
physical comfort.

He says, "I have to see the news."

She says, "Yes, but you're not watching it. You're not even listening." They kiss again.

He says, "I'll switch it off."

She says, "I'll make you some tea."

Neither of them moves. She arranges her limbs so they lie more neatly along his.

"Don't wriggle," he says. "You'll make me feel sexy."

After a while they rise unsteadily, pass the blaring television without noticing, and cross the room erratically towards the bedroom. Their progress is oddly slow, almost grotesque: one in front of the other, they prance across the room, pulling at clothes and clutching portions of each other's bodies—comic figures in an ancient frieze to celebrate some pagan festival: fertility or joy.

The late afternoon sun through the dark blue curtains sets the blue room quivering with underwater light. Their remaining clothes float away from them as they swim towards each other, weightless, giddy, fluent with desire. Their limbs dart and glimmer, merge and emerge, circle and twine. They are dazzled by each other's beauty, buoyant with their own wild sense of grace and lightness, silly with relief at their ease and freedom in this aqueous world. Amazed, once again, at these discoveries, her mind ripples ceaselessly against its mollusc thought: this is what I was made for. *This is what it is all about. This is what I am for.* And always, as they turn and flow into one another comes that glimpse, that glimmer of a roundness, a completeness in the other impossible to contain, impossible to grasp before drowning.

Subsiding at last on her ocean bed, the centre of her world, she stretches her limbs and finds the bed is curved exactly to their shape, opens her eyes on patterns of light set moving to her thoughts, and shadows of branches more tangled and mysterious than her dreams. Restored.

You recreate me on this bed of yours. You reconcile me to the world.

They eat high tea like children home from school: soft boiled eggs, hot buttered toast, ham and salad, toast and jam and tea. She tries to eat less than he, and fails. As usual. A low lamp they bought together glows golden as the darkness spreads outside, touching books and pictures, bowls of fruit and flowers.

"Everything I love is in this room," she says, trusting that he knows what is altogether too unlikely to explain: she means her statement without irony.

They drive across London in his little car and he drops her in a street at the back of the house she had left first thing that morning. The car is warm and dark and tight inside and the door must be wrenched open if she is to leave it. She gives him a nervous smile and wrenches at the door, climbs out and shuts the door imperfectly. She gives him a nervous wave and walks towards the corner. She will not look back. This time she will turn the corner, and not look back. She reaches the corner. She turns and looks for him. He hasn't vanished. He does exist. He is *there*. He smiles, and waves at her. Begins to drive away. She turns the corner. *Maybe he doesn't vanish when I'm out of sight. Perhaps I vanish when he's out of sight.*

Who knows? She moves solidly enough towards her house, opens the door, sails up in the lift, enters the flat with her key. Smells of cigarettes and whisky, sounds of transatlantic voices.

He's freshly barbered, wearing a new shirt, a new cravat, dispensing drinks and goodwill in the drawing room.

"Darling," he says. "You're late." And then: "My wife."

Two ageing San Francisco hippies and a smooth young New York lawyer shake her hand. The American panel for his well-known weekly television programme *Could it Happen Here?* He's warming them up before they meet the British team. "I said we'd take these chaps for some tandoori food. Would you believe they've never tasted it?"

She spills good humour, tolerance, even radiance over them. Perhaps they think she has a most fulfilling job. More likely they don't think of her at all.

He orders with his usual mixture of panache and greed. His sensuality is all for food. Decked like a bride's anatomy the food arrives. His guests must taste the flavours he has chosen for himself. His appetite transmits itself to everyone. She tries once more to eat less than the men, and fails. *If this goes on,* she thinks, *I will get fat. Among the other things I'll get, if this goes on.*

There are gaps between the men they cannot bridge. The hippies are largely non-verbal, the lawyer speaks legal jargon. They talk among themselves without exchange, as they eat the spicy food without absorbing flavour.

"Oscar Wilde said that England and America were two nations divided by a common language."

"No. It was Bernard Shaw."

There are only words, and silence.

He goes to bed the moment they get home and falls asleep before she has creamed her face. As always.

2

It was often hard for Sarah to remember what she had done with her life all those years before she had met Zack again, years when she had had only one marriage and had thought she was happy. She had been about to start on a book, she recalled, vaguely. *Emancipation '69*, or something, about the point women had reached, or rather hadn't reached, in their battle for human rights. Women's "consciousness" hadn't had much "raising" yet. After they met it hadn't seemed necessary, somehow, for her to do the book.

She always thought of that first meeting with Zack as when they had met *again*: they both seemed so sure they had once seen the other long ago for an instant they couldn't forget. This element of recognition was very strong for them. They knew that here was that person they had glimpsed, believed in, and awaited. It seemed that each of them had kept the image of the other alive through all the long years of adolescent fumblings, green marriages, and burgeoning domesticity, refusing to accept that such a radiant image should be allowed to fade with the many false radiances of childhood.

So in those first strange days when they had met and recognised each other, they talked the language of long lost lovers as they wandered through the private parks and enclosed gardens of the city while others were at work, and wondered that the sun shone every day, though summer was over.

"I used to kid myself, of course, that I could live without you."

"I used to wonder all the time what you were doing, and where you were."

They had to talk ceaselessly about their past because the unreal week had a natural ending: he had to catch a plane to a conference in Geneva. He telephoned her from the terminal and from the airport, and wrote to her on the plane. He said the sunshine of the week had lodged inside his head. He said her eyes had looked right into him, and always would. He said a lot of things. She kept his letters, postcards, notes, though she knew it was foolish and dangerous to do so.

That first day at their first lunch (the first of so many), it seemed to her they were marooned at their small table in the tiled vastnesses of the trattoria, and that the floor slid off for miles around them, empty of anything but echoes of themselves and their intensity. At the far corners of the restaurant, diners, one-dimensional as murals, sat pecking at their everyday lives. Excitement dried her tongue, filled her stomach, stimulated her bladder. When she stood up to go to the lavatory the stairs seemed to wind away from him for ever.

"You won't go away, will you?" she said. "You won't vanish. Promise me you'll still be here when I come back."

He was shocked by the panic he saw in her eyes. Could she not see his loneliness, his hunger, were as real as anything she had suffered in her past?

In those first days they did so many things which are forbidden, and did them far into the night, searching each other like explorers in a strange terrain. They laughed and were silent, hurt one another and were happy. They rode the waterbus from Westminster, sang songs in East End pubs, ate Beigels from an all-night bakery. They climbed to the top of a hill on Hampstead Heath in a fine and drenching rain. It was three in the morning. They climbed the seat they found there and danced on it, saluting the apathetic neon glow spread sullenly below. They lay in bed singing ancient pop songs for hours after they'd made love. Their voices were awful, especially hers, but their memories, combining, were prodigious.

They did the thing that lovers are forbid to do by law, by witches and by numbers: sometimes in their silences they'd look at one another and *say* they were happy.

Once, when they had been making love at night in their darkened room, she woke and saw him sitting on the side of the bed, his head in his hands. He had his back towards her and it shook. There seemed to be total silence in the room. About to exclaim, she sensed—with shock—that he was weeping. He made no sound at all. Shock silenced her and she lay rigid, pain and fear pulsating loudly in her blood. To know she couldn't help was very bad. To know she mustn't try to help was worse. Perhaps she would never know what springs of grief their tenderness had touched in him, nor why his silent weeping in the darkened room was intimate beyond the intimacies of any joyous thing they'd shared.

Sometimes they'd walk forgotten parts of London late at night. He'd show her areas she'd never seen. Crescents and streets and circuses unwound before her in the darkness like patterns in a blind man's eye. Canals and bridges, warehouses and parks: she had lived here all her life and never seen them. She had thought she had known the extent and variety of this, her city, as well as she knew herself. These revelations fascinated her and made her feel uneasy. She was avid to see more. These streets, these houses belonged to this place but to another time. They could not be part of the London she knew as she had known herself. Perhaps it was wrong to explore them, like walking among the dead, or on uncharted land? A light went on in an upstairs room at the end of a darkened street, confusing her further. People lived here still. People and ghosts together. She was frightened, but he led her on.

3

When Adam came back from New York she had not slept before four in the morning for more than ten days and friends were stopping her in the street to tell her she looked well. Even her secretary said she was looking rested. The skin was drawn tight across her face and blue marks glowed under her eyes. She wondered if he'd notice her strange radiance, as other people had. She wondered: would she leave him if he did?

He opened the door of the castle with his key and the image of what he would see there shone forcefully as ever in his familiar gaze. He knew he would find his castle as he had left it, everything in its place, as he had planned. And at its centre, by the hearth, she'd sit as she had always sat. In her place. Waiting. How convincing it was, his picture! How bright the colours! She looked at him and saw herself so clearly in his conviction, she could not look away. He had built this hearth and made this fire and put her beside it long ago. And there she would always stay.

Later, they lay side by side—not touching—in their huge four-poster bed. And he knew so surely that she lay

19

beside him (as the Queen lies by the King in the royal bed, in their castle he has built, in the parkland he has planted, in the country he controls) he did not need to put a hand out or to feel if she was there. So though her mind floated and her body burned. She was. There.

"Life is predictable with Adam."

"Of course it is," said Mel. "He makes the rules. And sees you keep them."

She was slapping paint viciously on walls.

"Should you be doing that?" asked Sarah. "If you *are* pregnant, it could bring it on."

"I've got to," said Mel. "I've got to get the attic fit to let, or we can't pay for the rest of the house."

Expensive door handles, bed-posts, mirrors, lay about the room. Downstairs were three more floors of un-inhabitable Lambeth gloom.

"Perhaps you should go into business," said Sarah. "Mel's Interiors. Domestic Bliss Guaranteed. Only impossible odds undertaken."

Sarah sat down on a step ladder and opened her brief-case. She took out a coffee jar of soup and searched for some papers at the bottom of the bag.

"And what's that?" asked Mel.

"*Bonne femme*. I saved some from last night for Zack. No point in making it, is there, if he can't have some too?"

"Fine flower of women's liberation you are," said Mel. "*Soupe à la bonne femme*—twice nightly."

"Shut up," said Sarah, who had found the papers she was looking for. "Okay, you can start complaining now about your plight. I'm going to interview you."

"I'm not complaining," said Mel. "I knew when I married Bill we didn't have the same tastes. We couldn't talk to each other. What I do mind is why does *he* mind me doing something I like when he's out doing something he likes? I mean if he's at football, or at the pub with the boys, why does he mind if I go to see a film, or come and see you? Does he really want me to sit by the 'phone *in case* he decides to ring up? In case he decides to want dinner at home? How could he ever have thought I was that kind of woman? I don't look like that kind of woman. He doesn't even like me doing voluntary work. 'One whole day a week,' he says. 'You could be doing something for me.' My back's hurting, and the pains are coming back. He should be here. He should be helping me." Mel sat on the floor and cried.

Later, when Sarah could leave her, she was leaving a white-faced child, straight hair scraped back, a good little girl alone in a large brass bounded bed in an empty room. She had had some whisky and a pill. She would sleep.

Typing her interviews was always a surprise. Sarah read:

```
That's what I opted for, you see. I
opted for sex. He's a marvellous lover,
and you can't have everything. I thought
I could do all the other things myself—
you know—read, think, learn, talk to
people.
And how does it work?
It would work better if I was pregnant.
```

She replaced the cover on the typewriter, replaced the jar of soup in her briefcase, and left the office. She passed a group of typists in the corridor.

```
My Mum says, there's nothing to it,
having a baby. It's just like going to
the lavatory, she says.
```

The flat was in darkness when she let herself in and Zack was sleeping on the sofa. She switched on a few low lamps and turned off the sound on the television set leaving the images flickering, then crept around quietly preparing some supper for him to eat later when she had gone. She hummed softly to herself, wondering at how lucky she was, not only that his flat was so near her office, but that the nature of his work, the pattern of his days, his week, fitted so neatly into hers.

Zack's day was divided between researching at the British Museum and lecturing at the University. The evenings were spent writing his mammoth work *The Persecution and Migration of Minority Groups: An Historical Perspective*. At the weekends, he himself migrated to the country, where his seventeenth century house and his wife Elizabeth awaited him. Their three children, aged thirteen, eighteen and twenty, were all away from home during term, at school or university, but Elizabeth seemed completely happy to spend days, and sometimes weeks, without her family, absorbed as she was in the house and garden, and most particularly these days in the kitchen garden where she cultivated the herbs she wrote about in her gardening and cookery books.

As Zack had a deadline, albeit an academic kind of deadline, on the first volume of his book and had promised to deliver it by the end of the year, he found it most conducive to work undisturbed each weekday evening at the flat where few people knew his telephone number, so that Sarah felt no great guilt at leaving him there alone. What she would have done had she fallen in love with someone who expected to spend the evenings with her, who made the usual practical demands, who forced decisions, she did not dare to think. Her only worry about Zack at that time concerned his students, whom she imagined ferociously nubile wherever female. She knew they were either frightened of Zack or adored him: sometimes both; and it was that dangerous combination she feared most.

"Look at those hags!" said Zack suddenly, startling her. "Look at those women! Witches, all of them." He had woken and was watching the soundless television screen where a group of women were arguing at a women's liberation demonstration.

"They look just like ordinary girls to me."

"Ordinary girls!" He shot her a scornful look. "With so much hatred in their faces? So much discontent?"

"You'd think they were the Bacchae," Sarah said.

"They are," said Zack.

"You liberal humanist professors! What are your reactionary, non-humanist ones like, I wonder?"

"Deist to a man," said Zack. "Worshippers at the shrine of the Eternal Female, be she White Goddess or Scarlet Woman, Blue Angel or Green Hat."

"Oh, Goddesses," sighed Sarah. "The pedestal, madam, or the funeral pyre? Reverence or contempt. Take your pick. You can be anything you like, madam, so long as it isn't human."

Zack's father had been killed in the last few weeks of the First World War, just before Zack had been born, so that he had been brought up, like so many men of his generation, entirely by women: mother, sisters, aunts. In his most formative years he lived in a world of female values, flourishing in the atmosphere of affection, sharing, unconsciously, the anxieties. His first year as a boarder at public school was the usual shock awakening to the brutal otherness of the exterior, masculine, world. He had become a man who liked women; loved them, admired and respected them and their achievements; but he looked for them always as he remembered them in that long ago womb world before school.

"A girl opened the door for me," he said suddenly. "Today. After class." Sarah said nothing. "I mean, held it open. For me to pass."

Sarah smiled. Good manners had been part of Mama's world: one opened doors for ladies. It was hard to think of some of those gutsy girl students as "ladies", but upbringing persisted.

"Age before beauty?" she suggested lightly.

"I don't know," said Zack. "I found it quite upsetting. Do you think they're frightened of me?"

"Of course they are. Deliciously, titillatingly frightened of you. So am I."

"That's altogether different," said Zack.

Before they left, he read her the pages he had worked on the night before, and as always she marvelled that he could make history so moving, so immediate. He identified to an extraordinary degree with each minority group he described, entering so intensely into their strange, forgotten lives that the sufferings he recorded might have been his own.

"Vivid *and* accurate," she pronounced, wishing that he, who could accept so much in life, could find it easier to accept her praise.

"Were you surprised to have survived the war?" she'd asked him once. He'd looked at her, puzzled.

"Perhaps you'd expected to be killed, like your father was?"

"I never thought of it like that, but I suppose you're right. Everything that happened afterwards seemed like a bonus. It was a bonus to be alive."

Driving beside him from one home towards the other she felt remorse and pity tug the tightrope in between: Adam alone and waiting now, Zack about to go back to the empty flat. What did she think she was—God's gift to man? Doling herself out in coffeespoons. She saw a long table crammed with all the people she loved most. Loaded with food and wine. She served dish after more delicious dish. She was serene, and smiled. Why isn't it possible to love and feed and talk to them under the same roof? How simple it would be. And how complex. We would all love each other in our different ways according to our needs. Time. Time is the great enemy of togetherness. We are strung along its wires like beads on an abacus. And I never learned to count.

She watched the car turn round and disappear, and stood for a moment alone in the dark square, watching the lights in separate lives go on and off, waiting for some coherent pattern to appear. The windows were symmetrical, rooms orange and comforting with light. Where do these strands of loneliness, these fitful interdependencies fit in? She tried to see the fragments separately but her mind recoiled like a spring into an old pattern.

4

"I was hungry," said Adam reproachfully, when she got in. "I had two apples and three bananas."

"But we're going out to dinner," said Sarah, appalled, as always. He told her what to wear and waited while she changed and did her face. He told her about his day.

They arrived at a large, well-lighted flat almost devoid of furniture. The host was an architect too fussy about design to commit himself by buying.

"And I still haven't got a wardrobe," Sarah heard the hostess saying. "Ten years of marriage, two kids, and nowhere to put my clothes."

"I've heard she tried to throw herself from the bathroom window," said Sarah, low voiced, to Adam. "Do you think that's why?"

"Not having a wardrobe, or not having a lover?" asked Adam.

"You know how it is these days," said Sarah. "No wardrobe, no lover."

They ate in a large and barren kitchen, all scrubbed pine and gleaming white machines. The other guests, impressed at meeting Adam whose face they had seen so many times on television, found the usual need to put him down. By scoring points off Adam they could feel level: he must be luckier than they, not—somehow—better. And knowing this, why then did Adam unfailingly get hurt? And Sarah, on seeing it, begin to swallow wine?

Halfway through the *gigot* by Elizabeth David out of Robert Carrier, they were both of them bored and drunk.

"The series may show that marriage doesn't work," Sarah heard herself declare.

"Marriages work because women make them work," said a tired-faced woman at the end of the table.

"Aha," said the host, re-entering the room with another bottle, "you're on to women's lib!"

"As an institution, marriage may be bad," said someone, "but it seems to be the best we've got."

"Like democracy. Three cheers!"

"Marriage is most often a state in which one person has a life and the other shares it," said Sarah.

"Bravo," said Adam.

"Still got the Aston Martin, Colin?"

"No, I've got a Jensen now."

"I agree with you," said the tired woman at the end of the table.

When they got home there were lights on and they could hear the television from the drawing-room. Suitcases were strewn about the hall.

"I hope you don't mind," said Mel. "The porter let me in."

She'd been crying through the late night film, leaving balls of screwed up tissues everywhere.

"Darling," said Sarah.

She made up the spare bed and tucked Mel in.

"What was it this time?" asked Adam. "Oh, it wasn't her fault at all. I know. It was all that sadist, Bill. Poor Bill. Has she asked you for any money yet?" He fell asleep.

They talked in the mornings after Adam had left for work.

"Why does it always have to be you who leaves? You who walks out with nothing and has to begin again?" said Sarah. "This town is full of homes you've made and then abandoned. Walls painted unlikely colours. Undistinguished rooms boasting odd relics of your style: Mel was happy here."

"I'd like to have stayed in the attic flat," said Mel. "He could have had the rest of the house. I have fantasies, you know, of me living on one floor of that house and Bill living on another and Jerry in the basement."

Jeremy was an old friend of Mel's and sometime lover. He had lived with Bill and Mel for several months and kept the peace between them. He was far more domesticated than Mel, bringing them tea and grapefruit and four-minute eggs in the mornings, and scoffing their thanks away by sending up his role as au pair boy.

"Very efficacious," he mocked, as he put down a carefully laid tray by the bedside.

"A cup of tea and you can face the day,

As my old auntie used to say.

A quick curtsey, darlings, and I'm off. Ta-ra."

Jeremy practised the trendy high-camp manner, but his face was the face of a sad, old-fashioned clown. He used his melancholy voice to make you laugh. He was an actor. He was sometimes queer. As the third member of a marriage he was invaluable. With delicacy he would disarm the combatants before the battle could begin; with humour he diffused the anger and dislike which grew between them, taking now one side, now another: keeping the balance.

"Now, Ada," he'd say to Mel, "leave the bloke some balls."

"Cool it, sweetheart," he'd say to Bill, removing the whisky bottle quietly.

One day he bought a houseboat with money he had saved and moved himself and his "bijoux" out. The war between Mel and Bill could rage unhindered.

"I could go and live with Jerry," said Mel. "Well, he's the only man I know who doesn't make demands. *Are* there any others, do you think?"

"Survivors," said Sarah.

"What?"

"Nothing. All men are difficult. Some are more difficult than others."

"With Jerry I can always be myself."

"Is that who you want to be?"

"Ooh, that was nasty." Mel pressed the button on the coffee grinder. The noise was deafening. When it stopped, Sarah said:

"Jerry doesn't cast you, doesn't give you a role. *He*'s the actor. Would you like so much freedom?"

Mel was silent. She was looking at herself reflected in the window. Branches of trees, chimneys and roofs and sky were reflected clearly in the image of her head. They were all the same size and seemed to be part of one another.

Sarah packed hard-boiled eggs and a jar of olives into her briefcase. She was going to make a salad for Zack. It would be hard-boiled eggs, tomatoes, anchovies and olives. They would eat it with new French bread. It would be good and Zack would be surprised.

Mel said: "We want independence, but we need to be needed."

Sarah said: "We think we should want independence. We want to be needed."

5

Leaving Mel uprooted in her kitchen every morning caused Sarah to wonder at those tangled roots which seemed to keep her firmly in the earth. Trees die standing up, she remembered. But the roots which held her so securely were not dead nor withering, though she had thought they might when she started so seriously to love Zack. People fell in love and left one another all the time. Yet she felt no desire to leave Adam. She could no more disentangle herself from him than unwrap her past. They had both been children when they met. Was it his fault she had grown into a woman? He had not been prepared for that contingency. It was not written anywhere in the story "And then she grew up." It was written only "They lived happily ever after."

Only now, with the confidence her new adult relationship with Zack had given her (it was, after all, the first time she had ever played the classic grown-up woman role to a grown-up man) did she dare to look squarely at the games she and Adam had been playing all these years. She tried to go back to the beginning.

In the beginning there was Adam.

It was as if at some point in his adolescence he had stopped thinking "I" and started thinking "We". Life before that had been a struggle between his parents and himself. Now he conceived of a much more general "them" against a self-contained new entity called "us". Accordingly, he looked around him to find a girl on whom he could impose the splendid vision of this unity. She must be a partner in his own image, a mirror reflection of himself and all his dreams. There would be no mystery about her, for what did one need to learn about so familiar a person as one's twin? He would tell her who she was. And when she had been told, they would become a pair, invincible against the world as long as they walked hand in hand through the forest, or slept side by side with the sword between them, or sat throne by throne like the kings and queens of fairy tales.

The first girl he met was too commonplace and did not understand his dreams, the second was too much interested in herself. But the third—it is always the third girl in the fairy tale—the third girl was trapped immediately by his need.

So there was never any question that his partner in life might be a person in her own right, or that she might have individual virtues and vices which did not take their source from him. If she excelled at some things, why, was it not expected of her as the reflection of such a brilliant man? Had he not created her in his own image, and written her every brilliance into the script? He would never understand her petty failings, her lateness, her untidiness, her habits of saving scraps of food, or carpet, and other unusable leftovers of domestic life. They were not, he reported in some bewilderment, in his plans. Had he left something out of the blueprint? Had the programming been incomplete? She had no sense of time, and freezing cold feet in bed.

She lived, though she did not know it, in his mirror, and unless they each developed along parallel lines, he could not see her at all. For a while they did so, and they recognised each other, but her belief in the importance of developing her own individuality and of realising, as far as possible, her own potential, took her into many places beyond the mirror which he would, had he heard her talk of them, have denied existence, like a man who believes that the world ends at the horizon.

He never saw her because he never looked at her. There was no need. He had ordained her appearance as he had ordained everything about her, and he relied on it. One had to assume things worked according to the rules. There was no need to listen, either, to what she said, for her answers must be faithful echoes of his own. He simply held out his hand without looking, and waited for her to put hers in it, which she always did. Hand in hand they walked down the streets of suburbs like children through the forest. She looked around her fearfully at the pebble-dashed houses crouched waiting to spring, the poison hanging from the laburnum trees, the evil hidden in privet hedges waiting to be revealed. She held more tightly to his hand. But his eyes were fixed firmly on the distance, where the path ran on into the glories of their future.

They had spent so many years now of the nine they had been married and the ones before that, plotting Adam's career which was to lead inexorably to that glorious future he saw more clearly and consistently than the present. It had been given priority over everything in their lives: it had been planned obsessively, and the plans had been doggedly carried out. He had dedicated himself to that sunrise in the distance, and dedicated her alongside him, so that she could not, eventually, think of it as his work, his life, but only as theirs, as indeed she had every right to: she too breathed the artificial air of the television world as if it were real.

He had identified himself so completely with his work, defined himself by it, that she could not rid herself of the idea: the work equals the man. Even now that he was well known and exposed to frequent attacks, she often found herself defending his opinions as fiercely as if she were defending he, himself.

It had only been in the last two or three years, after struggles and setbacks and the varying neuroses therefrom, that he had begun to be really successful. Their lives didn't change much, outwardly. They joked that now they could afford the standard of living to which they'd become accustomed. But she felt she had made a great investment of herself (enthusiasm? youth?) and would only now begin to reap rewards. If it had not been for the fortunate involvement in her own developing career she would have been in danger of becoming one of the deadliest by-products of affluent middle-class marriage: the vicarious career wife, a type who manifests her frustrations by pushing her husband's point of view insistently and with embarrassing sincerity in situations where he would rather not push his own.

"If I were a man," Isabel Burton had told her diary, just one hundred years before, "I would be Richard Burton. But as I am a woman, I will be Richard Burton's wife."

Her own work had grown up accidentally: it had not been part of his blueprint for their marriage. He hadn't known then of women's need to work. She'd worked, at first, of necessity, but gradually her jobs became more fulfilling, better paid. She accepted challenges, responsibilities. She took them on alone. He liked the money she brought in, grew to depend on it, and it was useful that she was kept too busy to get frustrated and complain about her lot as so many wives were doing. But as far as he was concerned, he worked, and she listened to him talk about his work, being helpful where she could. Whenever she wanted to talk about her work, or to ask his advice about problems she might have, she found he'd dismissed the subject and moved back to his own preoccupations. Angry at this one evening, she needled him:

"I've listened to you talking solidly for three quarters of an hour about your work. You know I'm interested, and I don't mind. I even like it. But you won't listen to

me talk about mine for five minutes. You say I'm grumbling, and switch off."

He was furious. Tight-lipped.

"Perhaps I'm more interesting," he said.

"And what's more, you believe he is," said Mel. "And
that he's more important, too."

6

The voice of a clarinet wound its way down the stairs
towards her, together with the smell of chickens basting
themselves in wine. She flew into the kitchen. Garlic and
herbs and wine could not obliterate that special smell of
him on her skin, in her hair. The oven had switched itself
on an hour ago while she had been in bed with Zack. She
sniffed her fingers. The food will be good tonight. I wish
I were making it for him.

```
     I found I could cope quite well with
  the sex angle. I mean making love to
  both in the same day. I thought I would
  be bothered about it, but I wasn't. As
  long as I manage to get home and bath
  and everything first. I couldn't cope at
  all if I couldn't have my bath, in
  between. You could say the moral thing
  had reduced itself to the washing bit
  with me.
```

She was bending over to put something in the oven
when the first of their guests came in. Paul Blake, an actor
and friend of many years.

"You're in a very vulnerable position, my dear," he
said, taking full advantage of the fact. When she

straightened up he pushed her against the sink and felt her up and down.

"Lovely body," he said. "Lovely bum."

She pushed him away, gave him a bowl of nuts to take into the other room, turned him towards the door.

"I'm not a monkey to be pacified with nuts." He re-appeared. "But if I were, I'd want to climb your tree."

She was busy again with salad and with garlic bread when Linda, Paul's wife, came in.

"Remember I thought I'd started the menopause," she said. "Well, I haven't."

"I should think not, at your age," said Sarah. "Put the fear of God into me, I can tell you."

Linda was one of the few women Sarah knew who seemed content as wife and mother, who seemed to use herself completely in these roles.

"I did feel a fool," said Linda. "I suppose I just wanted some attention for myself. You know how it is at home. Everything is Paul. Even when I had the baby he sat on the stairs being ill and I couldn't concentrate. I don't mind. I accepted it long ago—but it seems my body was rebelling. First I had gigantic spots on my legs before each period. Then I was sick regularly every Sunday night. Then I had a cold before each period, then really bad depressions every time. All that, and that's all it was —emotional!" She laughed as if she thought it funny.

During dinner they discussed the media with particular reference to television, films, acting and journalism, which happened to be the areas in which the gentlemen present worked. After dinner, Sarah cleared the dishes, and the women drifted one by one into the kitchen to talk about such trifles as their men and the upbringing of their children. When they were all there, Sarah said, "We might as well have withdrawn formally and left them to their port. Why does this always happen? Don't men ever talk about these things at all?"

In every city, every country she had lived in with Adam, the women had always gone into the kitchen to talk about anything that mattered to them. And to talk about it to each other.

They took the coffee back into the dining room. The men were discussing the media, with particular reference to television, films, acting and journalism.

"Where did you disappear to?" one said, suspiciously.

"Been grumbling about us, have you?" said another.

"Not grumbling," said Sarah. "Sharing experiences. We find it helps."

"Don't you ever discuss your personal lives at all?" asked another girl, emboldened by the solidarity of their kitchen conversation.

The gentlemen looked blank.

"Yes. With our wives," said one.

The wives looked blank.

"Hardly at all," said one.

The men went back to their talk of the real, external world. The women passed the coffee.

"Perhaps they don't have emotional lives," said Sarah. "Or so they would have us believe."

"No—as they would have each other believe," said Mel.

"The masculine world is a hierarchy based on power. Confess to a weakness—you go down a rung. Fakes and ladders." She giggled.

Mel could be clear about other people's lives, never about her own. She had moved in to Jeremy's houseboat and was busy making it a home. They had been to Paris for a kind of honeymoon, and now they were playing at being newlyweds. Sarah and Adam were commanded there for dinner.

There wasn't much scope for Mel the homemaker on Jeremy's boat because Jeremy had furnished and decorated it recently himself. So Mel was compensating by cooking the most difficult dish in the world. She had found the recipe in an eighteenth century cookbook, and had spent three days preparing it already. It seemed to need special unglazed ovenware which she had brought back with her from France, and they found her chopping chicken's livers for the second stuffing. While they drank and waited, Jeremy treated them to a concert in hi-fi; vocal flamenco so harsh it had to be authentic. Their ears longed for the seductive blandishments of an accompanying guitar, as he told them about his Spanish period of last year.

This year's "period" might be described as Stone Age Wholemeal, and was part of a movement which, while not exactly "back to nature" in the old simplistic sense, was certainly designed to put a primitive zest back into living. Jeremy was at pains to explain that it was not like vegetarianism, nor even macrobiotics, but nearer to the whole earth approach really, and after all, it was true that life was coming more and more packaged these days, wasn't it? Such revelations had caused his customary breezy camp humour to desert him and he went on to instruct them on the life-style of free-range hens, the humane slaughter of cattle, and the importance of breast feeding to humans in the same level tones.

His new helpmeet, who had naturally embraced his new philosophy with fervour, was to be heard from time to time cursing in the tiny kitchen as she filled the insides of wild ducks with brown unpolished rice.

"Hark at Ada," said Jerry, his sardonic manner returning briefly.

Sarah thought she detected suffering concealed in Jerry's masklike smile: of course! Forbearance! He wanted to be doing the meal himself. After all, *he* was the expert cook. They must have made a pact: Mel had to prove herself. There had to be something she could do to demonstrate that this time she was going to be happy.

For a short while they were visited by Desmond, a graphic designer from the neighbouring houseboat. Sarah recognised him instantly because he had always drawn himself: he had done a number of record sleeves in the late 'sixties, and in his style all four of the Beatles and many other stars had come to resemble Desmond to a remarkable degree. He was amazingly long and thin and amazingly pale. He wore rimless glasses and his ashen face finished in an impossibly long square chin. He was wearing a long narrow leather coat which he assured everyone was the genuine article got from an airman of the First World War who had worn it during combat.

There was something so two-dimensional about Desmond that Sarah had the disconcerting feeling that there was no back to his head, and that should she walk around him she would find notes on contemporary themes written on the cardboard of his back.

Jerry explained that he had been talking to Sarah and Adam about food pollution. Desmond looked longer and more solemn than ever.

"You just have to look at the Americans," he said earnestly. "You can see why they were in Vietnam. Because they eat beef. Nation of beef-eaters, you see. All that aggression. Builds up. It's got to go somewhere, hasn't it? Or take the Irish. Potatoes. All civil wars have been caused by staple diets—look what happened on potatoes. They have that effect on people. Of course, there's your intelligent potato and your unintelligent potato."

Adam put on his interviewing voice: "Really?" he drawled. "There could be *money* in *intell*igent potatoes. What, exactly, *is* an intelligent potato?"

Desmond was eager to expound: "An intelligent potato is a cooked potato. I never eat anything raw. It's not intelligent to eat raw food. The human race has become very passive. Have you noticed how passive it's become? I mean it just sits here, waiting. That's because the sun's dying. The moon's going to be the next sun. They're going to discover that quite soon—in about ten years

43

they'll discover that. It's draining all our energy, you see. Earth's turning into the new moon."

He vanished suddenly as if to demonstrate eclipse.

"Last time he was here he told me what mushrooms are," said Jeremy. "Do you know what mushrooms are?" Pause. "Apparently mushrooms are the sexual organs of fungi. The fungi are microscopic and live underground and they put out these amazing phallic structures so they can reproduce. Mushrooms are genitalia." He looked from Sarah to Adam gloomily. "It turned out to be true," he said. "I checked it out—and it was true."

When dinner was finally ready they'd drunk too much and were too tired to do more than taste its richness.

"You might at least look as if you're enjoying it," Mel flung at Adam.

"It's beautiful," said Adam gallantly. "I'm just tired, that's all."

"Tired, my eye," said Mel aggressively. "You disapprove, that's what. You've sided with Bill. I knew it all along. You see, Sarah, there's solidarity among men too—but only when their wives leave them."

"Shut up," said Sarah, terse and violent, while Jeremy looked round wildly wondering how one could exit from a houseboat without clanking carefully along the gang plank or jumping overboard.

"I'm not selfish," rasped Mel. "I know you think I am. I didn't want to hurt Bill. I need to be happy. Don't you see—happy?"

She began to cry. "At least I'm not like you . . . liberals . . . at least I don't wear fur or serve you bread that turns you blind—you have a chicken in my house you can be sure it had a *life*, strutted and squawked a bit before it had the knife put to its throat and all the blood spilled . . . out."

The ugly words choked her: she coughed, cried, beat her head on the table, her hair spilling into the rich mess of food.

They got up to go, Jeremy ushering them out, his face frozen.

"Put her to bed," Sarah whispered.

"Mop up her guilt," said Adam.

Jerry winced. "I'll cope," he said.

"At least I don't steal milk from calves," she screamed after them.

"Eaters of cruelty!"

Sarah couldn't sleep. She sat on the floor by the fire in the empty room, thinking of nothing. A dark square of window reflected within it a rectangular painting which in turn contained the cube of a window lit on the other side of the street. This arrangement of shapes seemed so complex, so perfect, she watched it in case it was a message. Snow began to fall. Because she was so seldom alone, she let the silence envelop her, feeling the layers of it: her thoughts encased in her body, her body in the silent room, the room in the sleeping house, the house in the snow-muffled square. Here we sit, she thought, with some amazement, inside ourselves, hardly listening, the emptiness walled in between us, one on top of the other, one next to the other, miles high, streets long. Prisoners.

She got up and went to the window. She wondered if she dared telephone to Zack. She pictured him sleeping in their blue room in that other square. The branches of trees were outlined now with snow, and the belisha beacon on the corner made amber patterns: on-off-on. A bowl of oranges floated surreal in mid-air reflected from her room. Why did that bowl of oranges suspended in space excite her more than the tangible fruit behind her? Why did that snatch of song she could hardly hear seem so much more haunting than any song she knew? When she turned, she was reflected five times round the room in different shapes and shadows. She began to pick at a hair growing on her chin. She wondered if anyone had noticed it. When I die hairs will go on growing on my chin, and the people who bury me will see them because then I won't be able to pull them out.

7

It seemed to be a time of departures. Adam went off to the U.S. again for another stint on *Could it Happen Here?* She had longed for his going so she could spend all her time with Zack. She had longed for a break in the round of restaurants and dinner parties, the ceaseless flow of demands, of activities. Yet when he left, she experienced his going as a sagging. The easing of tension does not always bring immediate relief: after balancing on the tightrope, there is the strange sensation of walking on the ground.

She moved in with Zack as she had dreamed of doing, and it seemed as natural as if she had lived with him all her life. They awoke together without surprise, and he brought her tea in bed in the mornings. But the emptiness of her other home disturbed her. She thought of the rooms there waiting cold and silent, and the thought reproached her. When she went there to see the maid, or meet someone, or collect some clothes, she switched on lamps and fires and watched the place come alive. Is that all it is, a home? A shutting of doors and a switching on of lights and fires, a curtaining of the dark?

Soon she had to prepare herself for the absence of Zack. He was going on a lecture tour of the Far East and would be away nine weeks. They avoided talking about it, but as the time came nearer, he had to prepare himself, had to make plans. When he had gone she wandered around for a few days, wondering which home to spend the evening in, which bed to sleep in, wondering who she should be now she had time to be herself.

There was time now for all the luxurious nonsenses of a woman alone. But what were the leisurely baths, the sensual body rubs, but preliminary indulgences to the greater indulgence of sex. It seemed typical of her life that the only time she had to do what women's magazines call "make herself desirable to the men in her life" was when they were neither of them there. "A woman needs time to herself", her mother had told her frequently in the past. Now Sarah wondered what she could have meant. And wondered too, not for the first time, how one could know so little of the person who bore one, so that their responsiveness, the areas of their sensuality, remained mysterious.

She took her mother to lunch. They sat opposite one another across a tiny table in an atmosphere of velvet and brocaded lights. In a hundred similar restaurants across London, people bared unmentionable psychic wounds at one another over the plump breasts of succulent *pigeons parisiennes* and washed down their sympathy with "une bonne bouteille", but Sarah's mother talked about possessions: possessions she had, possessions she wanted, possessions her daughter ought to have. Sarah ordered the food and wine in a spirit of benevolence. She was comforted by the thought that, however generous her giving, it could not be possessed. By tomorrow morning at the latest, the possessors would be largely dispossessed.

"One thing about your father," her mother was saying. "I only have to ask." She looked moistly at Sarah over the rich food.

Meaning you always know how to get what you want, thought Sarah. You always have. The first law of survival. In which I am deficient.

"Does he mind you being out for lunch?"

"No, I don't think so. I left him a tray with everything. All he has to do is boil himself an egg."

"It's all he can do, as I remember."

"He's getting better now."

"You mean he makes the tea?"

They laughed.

"It's just that since he's retired, he's—well—he's *there* all the time," said her mother. "Every time I talk on the 'phone he wants to know what kept me so long. When I go to the hairdresser he says, "But, again? You were there last week.""

All those years getting used to spending the days alone. Filling your time. Trying not to be hurt by absence, by separation. Then just when you've managed some kind of shaky independence, they retire, and everything changes.

"You have to begin again," said her mother.

"We're always beginning again," said Sarah.

"Perhaps it's a good thing. At least we're adaptable."

Work equals independence equals some kind of freedom, thought Sarah. She wanted to say: "Mum, have you ever loved a man other than Dad? I mean, is he the only man you've ever been to bed with, all your life?" She'd come right out with it. Why not? "Mother," she'd say, "have you ever had a lover?"

"Oh," said her mother, "look! Fresh pineapple. My favourite. Ooh, do you think I could?"

Well, my sister telephoned and said I
think you'd better go and see Mum. I
hadn't been there for a few weeks. And
when I got there, she was sitting in the
front room with the curtains drawn in
broad daylight, with all the fires on,
shivering. And scratching and scratching
at her arm. It was bleeding over my
father's desk. I think she must have
been doing it for weeks. Oh yes, my
father was there, upstairs. He's never
been any good at that kind of thing, so
he justs gets on with his work. I think
it must have started after my sister
left home. With both her little
fledglings gone, she'd nothing to live
for, I suppose.

She had drinks with several people she never had time to have drinks with, allowed herself a couple of mild flirtations, had to throw one of Adam's best friends out of the flat and lock the door. He telephoned her five minutes later from a call box round the corner. "I just wanted to tell you that was only the first round," he said.

She went to a party given by a hermaphrodite friend and met a coloured foot fetishist (male) who drooled over her sandalled toes. At Paul and Linda's she met a thin young man who was studying at the Sorbonne and acting as a courier in the summer. He told her she was a witch, so she went to the cinema with him and asked him up for coffee. They talked until two in the morning. At about midnight the street doorbell rang and they sat petrified, staring at one another as if they had been caught making love. If she answered the bell and some of her friends came up, who would believe they had been discussing the philosophy of travel, the futility of searching for meanings in foreign countries other than the self?

Admiringly, he told her she had the best mind he'd encountered. In a woman. "That's a pretty insulting thing to say," she told him, "to a woman." Laughing, she pushed him, too, out of the door.

When Adam came back from New York he seemed larger and glossier than his screen image. He had had his greatest success ever with six programmes on the "woman movement" in which he'd featured every bright lady in the news and every card-carrying male chauvinist he could find. The resulting fireworks had been dubbed "dynamic television" by *Variety* and he was now Sir Knight. It was hard to settle down with this celebrity: the telephone rang all the time and breathless girl reporters turned up for interviews. "As we all know, nothing succeeds in New York like success," he told Sarah. "The place is built on it, designed for it: it just swings into action."

He wandered round the flat restlessly. "It seems so small," he said. He picked up some of Sarah's things from his chest of drawers and thrust them at her. "I live here, too," he told her. "It's not as tidy here as an hotel."

She was absurdly hurt. "I should think not. It's a home," she said.

Groups of people he'd met turned up to dinner all the time: Washington hostesses, southern senators, a Red Indian princess, several smashed Los Angeles love children, a pair of lesbians who had left their husbands and adopted lesbianism as a cause. A fascinating kaleidoscope of people, and she longed to talk to them all in a leisurely manner, even to interview some of them herself, but just as they started to warm to her, she had to go and prepare the dinner. She began to detect a disquieting impulse in herself: after a while she needed to tell them about her job so that they would not think she was simply a wife. To be fair, most of them knew what she did, for Adam had told them, but the odd ambivalence in her attitude persisted.

Everyone told her how lucky she was to have such an understanding husband. We were so impressed, they all told her: he really empathises. It's amazing. For a man.

The final straw came when her own paper sent someone to interview him and the journalist, an old colleague of Sarah's, asked her "What's it like being married to such a liberated man?"

"How should I know?" she muttered, having just discovered that all that morning's post and the papers had been opened by Adam, looked at, and thrown away.

During his absences she kept everything which might be of interest to him, religiously clipping newspaper items, filing circulars. That evening at midnight, he switched off all the lights in the flat when he went to bed, having failed to notice Sarah was still up. "Lucky, am I?" she muttered, groping her way blindly to bed down the darkened passage.

Fortunately, she was in the process of decorating Zack's flat at this time, while Zack was away, and this was a pastime which gave her pleasure out of all proportion to the effects. She was absolutely sure about what she chose: she knew Zack would like it. He had left her some money and told her to do as she pleased. For the first time she felt herself truly in charge, mistress of the house in a way she had never been with Adam, for there she could never choose anything that had not been ordained. Adam made the decisions and expected her to carry them out. She was consulted formally, so that she could not complain. And so now, with Zack's flat, she indulged herself in a Mel-like orgy of homemaking, endlessly planning the minutest detail for Zack's comfort and contriving it so he could not fail to feel the hot breath of her caring all around him.

All the same, she began to get desperate without him. His letters were bleak with loneliness and fatigue and that curious strain of moving from one place to another too fast. The balance was upset: she listened to Adam all the time and nobody listened to her. She began to feel she would go slightly mad if she couldn't reach Zack, if she couldn't reassure him she was here on the same planet, though each day presented fresh evidence to the contrary. Stifling her considerable supply of common-sense, she sent him an embarrassing cable which was read out to him over the telephone in his Tokyo hotel in a clipped Japanese accent. Not content with this, she tried to telephone him at some university he was scheduled at, but she got the organiser and had to pass a message. It was an extremely odd message. She had heard of an aircrash and hadn't slept properly for several days.

I had this best friend at school. She was very artistic. Not just in a dilettante way. She had a small but genuine talent, and she wanted to be a sculptress. She was one, I suppose. Her work was quite interesting. She married a farmer straight from school and she tried very hard to be a farmer's wife. Their farm was in a really remote place miles from anywhere and they were surrounded by the kind of natural objects she used for her work. For a while it worked, but then she had three babies one after the other in a row and it wore her out. It was just too much for her and she felt she couldn't cope, what with the farm and everything. She wasn't very strong at the best of times.

He would come home from the fields and find her sitting in the middle of the three children, all four of them sobbing uncontrollably. He was amazed. He thought she ought to be happy. He thought: she's my wife, she's a mother, she'll snap out of it.

She took one of his guns and loaded it and she went to a platform over the river where the salmon jump and she shot herself through the mouth.

It was lucky she didn't make more of a mess of it, really: she'd forgotten she wore a dental plate in her mouth and the shot might not have killed her but wounded her brain. It would have been terrible if she'd lived horribly paralysed. She must have thought she would fall into the river and if the shot didn't kill her, she would drown. But she didn't. She died there on the platform overlooking the valley. I often think of her there, surrounded by winter fields, and trees curving bare over the skyline like some of the drawings she used to do at school.

8

Sarah and Miles had to go to see the proprietor of their newspaper to discuss the series. He was an old man who had recently been ill, and was living at present on his farm in the country. They drove out on the motorway, then left it for a network of high-hedged lanes. When they got to the farm it was twilight and a bitter wind blew round the dark edges of barns. Stable doors creaked, and as they got out of the car, the snow which had been threatening all day began to fall in earnest.

The old man brought them to the fire and offered them tea or wine. Craving a cup of tea, Sarah opted for wine, which she knew the men preferred. The discussion went quite well, the old man being shrewd and lively. He was interested in the subject of marriage, having been married three times himself, and set up a number of mistresses in his time. Who could guess he would be dead within the year?

They looked out at the farm, now covered with the new white of snow and at the line of barn roofs and trees against the sky. The old man had brought out a special bottle of Scotch. Sarah declined in favour of more wine. "Too good for women, anyway," said Miles. The old man cackled into the fire.

"You can stay tonight, if you like," he said, looking from Miles to Sarah. "Plenty of room. It might be a difficult drive to London if this keeps up. Could get stuck in a drift, y'know."

She could see Miles consider: can I seduce her here, under the old man's roof? He came to a decision. Walked to the window. Ran his banana fingers through his carrot hair. Turned and grinned his malicious melon grin. "It's all that virgin snow, sir. Can't wait to make my mark in it."

"He, he, he," said the old man. "He, he, he."

It was pitch black when they started back and the car skidded as they swung into the lane.

"Wine doesn't help," said Miles cheerfully. "But you do."

With his spare arm he pulled her across the seat until she was sitting up against his haunch. For such a weedy, unco-ordinated person, he was extraordinarily strong.

"Mind what you're doing," she gasped, as they hit a snow covered post and careered into another narrow lane.

"I know what I'm doing," said Miles, as he squeezed her breast.

She put his hands on the wheel and they crept on, the noise of the windscreen wipers and the arc of the head-lights isolating them from the silent darkness around them as surely as if they had chosen to be together.

"We could get stuck in a snow drift," said Miles. "I'd like to get stuck in a snowdrift with you."

"Just drive," said Sarah.

He grabbed her hand and put it on his thigh.

"I could fuck you in a snowdrift. I bet you've never been fucked in a snowdrift."

"Keep moving," said Sarah. "We've got to keep moving."

"Who cares if we never reach London?" said Miles.

"Keep your hand on the wheel. No, *both* of them. It could be *dangerous*," she said.

A car in front of them skidded and Miles slowed down further just in time. They were doing a steady ten miles an hour, and the thickness of the snowflakes had muffled the world outside the car so that only the black barks of trees at the side of the road existed, only the thump, thump, thump of the windscreen wipers against the unaccustomed weight of snow. It was eery and beautiful and silent.

"Put your hand on my cock," said Miles.

"Oh, for God's sake," said Sarah, "that *would* be sensible. You've got to concentrate. Just keep going."

They moved slower than a big river down the centre of a motorway, dimly aware of patterns of light through a blur of snow and water.

"You'd always remember it. In a snowdrift. It would be something you'd remember when you are old."

"Because it was cold," said Sarah. "I'd remember it because it was cold."

"Got to have a pee," said Miles.

He got out and went behind a tree. Absolute silence enveloped her. She fell into a dream. And became aware of shouting going on somewhere outside the car's warm fug. Miles was gesticulating, trying to catch her attention. He was holding a thick, black iron bar about two feet long. He had picked it up from the snow.

"Look," he was shouting, when she got the window down. "Look! It's fallen off!" He seemed jubilant. He did a little dance, pointing at his crutch.

"No need to worry now, little Sarah," he said, as he climbed back into the car. "It's fallen off with the cold."

And a little later, sadly: "It fell off because you didn't want it."

"More likely the cold," said Sarah.

9

When she got home she was trembling with relief and cold, but before she could boil a kettle, the telephone rang. It was Adam. He was at the studio doing a recording. He had to tell her Jeremy had rung. It was Mel. She'd taken a lot of pills. They were pumping her out. He thought she'd want to know.

The hospital was dark like the gothic nightmare it is not supposed to be. She went up in the service lift. There were shapes in the lift—bales? stretchers? people?—she didn't dare to look. Shaking herself for cowardice, and glancing briefly round, she saw Jeremy standing in the corner, waiting for the lift to go down again. He was raincoated, belted, hunched. He wouldn't meet her eye.

She got out on the top floor and was greeted coldly by a neat, young nurse. "You can't go in now. They're changing her blood," she said. "Are you a relative?" She disapproved. Wasting the resources of this hospital on people who want to draw attention to themselves. Sarah peered through the windows and saw Mel propped up, beached like some flimsy giant fish, her hands bigger than her arms, her arms whiter than the sheets. They were doing something with bottles and wires and plugs.

"You're still plugged in," Sarah said, when they let her in. *Be flippant, otherwise you'll cry.* Mel looked defiant.

"You didn't want to die, did you?" said Sarah.

About to say, "Yes, I did," Mel glanced at Sarah's face. "I don't know," she whispered, blinking rapidly. She smiled, a small, defeated smile. "I don't suppose I did."

Waiting outside again, Sarah sat by a sun-lounge window surrounded by wheelchairs and dying potted plants. The smell of decay and disinfectant suffocated her, made her feel sick.

How strange it was, Mel hadn't died, and yet she seemed defeated.

"She was full of the stuff," she heard the nurses say.

"Can't do this to yourself too many times," they said.

"Effects? Oh, it had its effects. On the system. Yes. Oh, yes. You don't get off scot-free."

She had tried to kill herself. Mel. She had wanted to die.

Part Two

I

She went up the steps of an elegant Victorian house and rang the bell. For a long time there was no answering sound, and at last, Sarah, who had been preoccupied, as always, with her own thoughts, began to realise it was oddly quiet for a place that housed six children and attendant adults. Then she heard a kind of muffled thud, the door swung open and the tall figure of Jonathan B. confronted her, a bemused expression on his face.

"Oh, Sarah, it's you. Come in," he said politely. He was looking at her in a dazed, unfocussed way. "Have you been ringing long? I was working . . . at the top of the house . . ." he gestured. "I didn't hear the bell."

He must have taken the stairs three at a time and jumped the last six, hence the thud she had heard. His shirt was open to the waist, and his hair stood up from constant fingering. There was a certain aloof radiance about him: he was writing a new play and it was going well. There was a sheen of moisture on his chest and at the roots of his thick fair hair, and as he ushered her into the drawing room, Sarah caught the smell of sweat on silk.

Alarmed by this new, vital, working Jonathan, so different from the languid young success she'd met at parties, or seen in TV interviews, Sarah asked hurriedly, "Where's Miranda? Today was the day we fixed for me to do her interview."

"Oh, God," said Jonathan, pouring Scotch and adding ice to it. "She's gone away. Gone to her mother's. Taken all the kids. They went last week. She must have forgotten. Not like her at all."

He pressed a switch and, note by note, the music of an unaccompanied guitar crept down from his attic workroom to where they stood in cool half-curtained gloom, ice clinking as they drank.

"I was such a swine . . ." He paced around. "Those last few days . . . you can't imagine . . . all those children in the house . . ."

"And now . . . ?"

"Well, now it's moving, anyway," he said. "I'm into the third act. Three or four days at a stretch makes all the difference . . . peace and quiet . . ."

"I must go," said Sarah. "Let you get on."

"No, no. Not now you're here. Stay. You can do an interview with me. The husband's point of view. I bet you haven't got much of that! After all, I have been married twice, and our six kids are an assorted bunch, one mine, three hers, two ours."

Jonathan B., famous for loathing journalists, persuading her to interview him!

"Well, now I've interrupted you, let me at least make you some lunch," said Sarah.

"I can open a can with the best of them," he said.

She followed him into the kitchen where she watched him open a tin of oyster soup and a bottle of burgundy. He poured the soup into bowls, the wine into goblets, set them all on a tray, added a tin of Bath Olivers, and, weaving slightly, carried the tray back into the drawing room.

They sat together on a low sofa, the soup bowls on a table by their knees, goblets in hand. Sarah set her tape recorder, and he talked, the notes of the unseen guitar keeping the difficult words apart from one another: love, dependency, marriage, pain. His guilt at leaving his first wife; his concern for Miranda; his determination that the children shouldn't suffer; his fear that he might fail to support them all on what he called "the fragile spinnings of my feeble brain". An unexpected gentleness emerged from these complexities; Sarah was moved by it.

"Jonathan," she said, "have your soup. It's getting cold." She patted his hand, but his skin burned her. He leaned across to fill her glass and kisses, lighter than shadows, patterned her temple and her cheek. They talked. He kissed her mouth, she kissed his, and still they talked.

"Shall we go to bed?" he said.

She leaned against him, gathering strength to make the weary climb away, strength to say "no" because "no" was what she always said, what she always wanted to say.

The warmth of his body permeated hers. "I feel safe," she said, drowsily, wondering why.

She held his head in her hands. "What a heavy head!"

"Must be the brains."

They kissed again, their mouths fitting perfectly, softness on softness.

Supposing, for once, I don't want to say no?

The thought was like clouds clearing, like curtains opening. It cleared her of all other thoughts. She stared at him in surprise. He spread her hair around them both and knocked gently at her head.

"What's going on in there?" he asked.

Up deeply carpeted stairs he led her, past beds and bedrooms of every shape and size, up into the sky. His workroom was quite bare, and stretched across the house with windows at each end. A desk, a chair, a lamp, a typewriter. A large bed with a patchwork quilt. They lay together on the patchwork quilt and were gay and tender with one another, as if they believed that love could be this easy, this lighthearted, the carefree business of a Wednesday afternoon.

Later, she fled past mirrors reflecting angles of her nakedness, into the bathroom he had directed her to use. Miranda's bathroom: dark, luxurious, ornate, the sunken bath fringed with a long-haired carpet, ankle deep. Sarah sat on the bidet, mindlessly humming as she plied the soap. A gobbet of matter, large and a clear, deep red, swam in the swirling water. Horrified, she stopped the flow and stared at it. Not hers. She checked herself. No, not today, it couldn't be. Well, whose? Another woman here today? Last night? Miranda had been away for several days. Could it have stuck to the rim of the bidet and been only now flushed out? The brightness of its red astounded her. She turned on the taps to finish washing, and watched it disappear.

The radio blared in the car he had ordered to take her home, and the driver insisted on talking all the way. It had been raining, and the river road was shiny as black glass. Reflections.

Patterns of light from all those windows lacing their bodies as they moved together on the bed in that bare room.

His weight.

The things he'd said.

"What do you see," she'd asked, as they looked, like lovers, into one another's eyes.

"Only myself," he said.

Reflections.

2

Mel waited outside the hospital, her thin body drawn up tautly against the wind, her head on its long stalk peering angrily into the day.

"Where have you been?" she said, accusingly. "You've got to get me out of here. Do you know where I am? In the *mental* ward. I'm not *mad*, you know. If you try to take your life, they think you must be mad. They're crazy in there, all of them."

They walked along the river and across a newly painted bridge, the wind tugging at them.

"Never mind," said Sarah, her face in the sun. "I'll talk to them. I'll fix it, don't worry. I'll get Adam to write a letter. We'll get them to say you can come and stay with us."

She smiled to herself and leaned her body into the wind, feeling the strong, swift pull of the river as it flowed beneath them.

"You're happy," said Mel, suspiciously. "What's up?"

"Can't I be happy?" Sarah spread her arms out wide and spun along the bridge, hair flying. "It's a nice day, hadn't you noticed?"

Sun on water. Spring coming. Reflections.

The pale, tense face watched her resentfully.

"I can't go back to Bill. I can't go back to Jeremy. I can't go back," said Mel.

Sarah hugged her, shocked at the lightness of Mel's skinny frame. "It'll be all right. You'll stay with us. It will be like old times. You'll see."

The sun in her eyes obscured the look in Mel's.

I had to have this cauterising done, you see. I'd had this trouble ever since I'd had the children, but I never had time to have it seen to. No, it doesn't hurt. It's just a bit unpleasant, being strapped up like that and having that clamp screwed on. And it is a bit frightening seeing smoke coming out from in between your legs. They don't give you an anaesthetic because you don't need it: the place they actually burn is not sensitive, you see. But in the evening, I did feel very tired—my back ached—and I'd quarrelled with him and we hadn't spoken to each other for a week, so he wouldn't help me with the washing up and I nearly collapsed before I'd finished it. The washing up? Oh, I had to do it. I couldn't leave it. The next day was the au pair's day off, and I'd just have had more to do in the end. . .
You're not supposed to have sex for six weeks after this thing. That'll really drive him round the bend. It was me not wanting it before that caused the quarrel. . .

So Mel moved into the spare room again, and she and Sarah had breakfast together in the kitchen every morning when Adam had left for work. Sometimes Mel talked astrology and told their fates and fortunes. Sometimes she consulted I Ching, or played the tarot cards.

"We should have had families at school, by now," she said. "Do you remember how, when *we* were at school, we used to plan our lives? What we'd be doing when we were twenty, or some unimaginable age like twenty-five? How many boys or girls we'd have? And look at me: two broken marriages, a string of sad affairs, and an unstable womb."

They played ridiculous games with titles, singing and dancing about like a couple of fools:
"A womb with a view
    And you . . ."
Blue Womb; No Womb at the Inn; the Womb is Full; A Womb of One's Own; Just a Womb at Twilight; Other Voices Other Wombs. No prizes were given for the worst, but when the games were over, Mel became silent with a new kind of silence which frightened Sarah. Images of the mental ward would surface in her memory and they'd look at them together: the hospital's obsession with physical cleanliness and order; the lining up of beds—co-ordinated beds for unco-ordinated people; the patients' rota for the polishing of floors; the dribbling, the shambling and the giggling, skirts up and knickers off in the formal gardens.

For the first time in their long friendship, Mel seemed out of reach to Sarah: often now she would start some metaphysical flight which took her into realms beyond nonsense where Sarah could not follow her and she ended hunched up and alone, in tears.

Not wanting to leave her alone too much, Sarah took her to the office, where she met Miles.

"Don't pester her," Sarah warned him. "Mel's given up men."

"She can't," said Miles. "She hasn't tried me."

"They all take you for granted in the end," said Mel.

"I wouldn't," said Miles.

"That's what they all say at the beginning," Mel told him. "But when you live with them for a bit, you discover what their priorities really are: drinking, working, gambling, horses, football, eating, reading, watching television. And somewhere after that come wives and mistresses."

At the end of the list comes love.

"I always put women first," said Miles.

"You always put fucking first," said Sarah.

"My trouble is, I've never had a mistress who gave me priority as I did her," said Miles. "I always came after dinner parties for neighbours, tea parties for children, drinks on Sunday mornings, evenings at the launderette . . ."

A friendly journalist who'd been listening, laughed and said: "As long as you always came, Miles. As long as you always came."

"Piss off," said Miles. "I'm planning a seduction."

"We should be able to come to some arrangement, you and I," he said to Mel. "We both want someone who'll put us first."

"After you," he said, gallantly, ushering her before him so he could pinch her bottom as she left.

"You can't expect anything but pretentions from a girl whose mother named her Mélisande," said Mel.

She was learning to crochet. Balls of coloured wool lay about the flat. Adam collected them in his tidy way, but they reappeared again mysteriously.

"And who and where is Pelléas?" he enquired, distastefully examining a shapeless garment she had made.

"It was supposed to be romantic," Mel said. "*I* was supposed to be romantic. Beautiful and romantic, because my mother was beautiful and romantic, and nothing came of it. She married my father, and sacrificed everything for me. So *I* had to make better use of *my* assets— my name and her beauty. I had to, because she didn't."

"And what does *that* mean?" said Adam, with sudden and surprising sharpness. "Finding a better man than your father? Finding a one hundred per cent failure-proof man, the all-purpose, all-weather husband, never lets you down, lives up to every dream, guaranteed safe in every storm. It never occurred to you, I suppose, that you could develop resources of your own to make yourself happy, like a man has to most of the time?"

"But those were supposed to *be* her resources," Sarah pointed out. "According to her mother, that is. One had assets, if one was a woman, not resources. Goods and chattels have assets, people have resources. Her beauty

74

and romantic nature were assets which were supposed to buy happiness."

As Sarah finished this speech, the phrase "feminine viewpoint" could be heard from the television, and a female voice started to speak. At once, the two girls who had not watched all evening, turned their faces to the screen.

"Marvellous!" said Adam. "Can you imagine a man showing interest just because another *man* came on? Yet one supposes there are as many and varied and different women in the world as there are men." He scratched his thinning head. "Probably more. Half the world is female. At least half. Can so many feel this solidarity? What is this sisterhood?"

"The sisterhood of the oppressed," said Sarah gaily, as she and Mel went into the kitchen to prepare the supper.

```
     I was only eighteen when he married
me, and I'd had a very sheltered life
and no one had told me anything about
marriage. Or about anything. I was
fearfully romantic. He used to stand by
the bed every night and say: Do you
think I should bother to put my pyjamas
on? I didn't know anything about sex.
And when it happened I thought it was
awful. I just gritted my teeth, I
suppose, like some ghastly Victorian. I
just bore it. And I had a dreadful time
having the kids. It was really hell. I
was awfully bad at it. I'm full of
stretch marks and things, and my body's
ruined. I spent years thinking I could
```

never be attractive, or good in bed or
anything. He used to stand by the bed
and say: What do you want me to do, tie
a knot in it? Then I met S. He made me
feel like a woman. Quite honestly, sex
is much better with my husband now I've
realised I don't love him.

The streets were full of children. They seemed to be
everywhere, playing leapfrog or hopscotch or some other
ancient pavement game. Strange that she had not noticed
them before. Once she saw two small fair-haired boys
perched on a scarlet pillar-box like leggy emblems,
signifying something.

When she got back to the office, Mel had telephoned.
She rang her back and heard some nonsense about
"messages". Five minutes later, something clicked. She
never was sure exactly what it was. She leapt into a taxi
and headed for home again. She opened the door and
marched through the flat like a Fury.

"What have you done?" she yelled.

Mel was hunched up and sheepish, lying on her bed
clutching a towel.

"Cut your wrists, haven't you? I might have known."

She pulled Mel harshly to her feet and led her, wrists
together, to the kitchen sink. Water flowed fiercely over
the two pale slits she had made, and the veins stood out,
strongly blue in her white skin, their intricacies unbroken.
There was hardly any blood.

"How could you?" Sarah shouted. "How could you
do this to me? And in my flat, too? Don't you know how
I'd feel about it—afterwards?"

Mel wept. "I didn't cut them much," she sobbed. "I didn't dare. It wasn't very deep."

Sarah stuck two plasters tightly on her wrists and marched her into the living room. She put her in a chair and poured two brandies.

"Here, drink this."

Her hands trembled with anger. They sat silently, swallowing brandy without comfort. Sarah rocking herself without rhythm, Mel in some place beyond words.

"What will I ever do with you?" said Sarah.

"I love you very much," said Mel. And then: "I think I'll go away."

I never expected to be stuck out in the suburbs with two kids waiting for my husband to come home. It's just not me. I visualised—oh, I don't know what I imagined when I first came down to London and started modelling and became successful. It was all unreal. I was afraid I'd wake up one morning looking ugly and it would all be over. Cinderella in reverse. He was very powerful and successful when I met him and by the time we married he was getting rich, too. I'd always wanted to be rich, but it doesn't seem to have made us happy the way it's meant to; I still can't go out and buy a dress without feeling guilty. And I stay here all day looking after the kids and try incredibly hard to keep myself—and the children and the house—looking

glamorous, and God knows, it's a sweat,
and I wait for him to come home and
appreciate us. But he's so fagged out
when he does come home he doesn't want
to know about the kids or anything—and
all he does is tell them to shut up and
go to bed when they've been waiting up
all evening just to see him . . . All he
wants, really, is to flop down in front
of the telly. And if the house isn't run
as efficiently as his bloody office, he
complains to me. It's not a home for
him, this place—and I try to make it a
home. It's just an extension of his
office which isn't half as slick. And
I'm an un-super inefficient secretary
extension.

Mel enrolled at some Adult Educational establishment
attached to a university in Wales.

"A degree course. Social Sciences," she told Sarah.

"Just when you need me most, you go away."

"I'll be all right," said Mel.

In an ancient car, piled up with books and pots and
pans, they drove to the station. Mel wore a purple smock,
her hair tied back, legs bare. Sarah watched as the pale
dancer's calves disappeared into the sombre red brick
building. Such a vulnerable glimmer of pale flesh. For
some reason she couldn't fathom, she thought of Stanley
Spencer's women, and the way he painted flesh. And of
Zack. Always of Zack. Of Ella singing "Everytime we
say Goodbye". That voice, aching, but singing. Liquid
loneliness.

> When you're near
> There's such an air
> Of spring
> About it . . .

Sarah hummed the slow melody in double quick time, making herself walk briskly along the damp pavements, as she often did when she felt she was losing: as if to pretend that her purposeful movements and the time gained by their speed could somehow compensate for her unconstructive thoughts. It was the same curious need which compelled her to tidy drawers and cupboards when her period was due: as if she could balance such everyday achievements against the monthly loss.

Her strides marched her across a line of tiny school-girls queueing for a charabanc, pushing one of them out of place. The child, a little chocolate-coloured girl, began to cry; Sarah knelt down, cuddled her, and put her back in line. For a moment she held the sturdy brown curves of this child's body against her own, and yet that moment's contact dried the snuffles of the child, and filled her arms so naturally she wondered what she'd used them for before.

She watched the children climb into the coach and as it moved away her little friend detached one pudgy hand from the rail, and, balancing precariously, waved to her. What did she see, this solemn child, in the face of the lady on the pavement?

A childhood image—dream or memory?—recurred to

Sarah: six years old and unobserved, she stood on a pavement and watched her mother go past her on a bus. Sharply, with shock and guilt, she saw the expression on that necessary face which had now become Other—a strange and private face. *She* knew her mother was young and beautiful, animated, gay; yet the face glimpsed through the window of the bus seemed set in sadness.

3

When Zack came back at last and they made love again
and she lay becalmed, she was tricked by her happiness
into that old and foolish thought: that she could say
anything without danger.

"Everything will be the same only better," she
announced aloud to the moving patterns of light on the
wall of their blue room as one who casts her spell upon
waters.

"I'm afraid it won't," said Zack. "Nothing's ever the
same. You see, Japan was such a success, I've been asked
to go back next year. Head a mission there. Research.
Migrations of different groups of workers. Treatment of
minority groups. It's a year's project and means travelling
all over. Are you going to come with me?" he asked.

*So this is how the world ends. Not with a bang or a whimper.
Just a man and a woman lying on tangled sheets, planning the
future.*

They made love again, and bathed and dressed and ate
their sumptuous tea. The newly decorated flat glowed
like a jewel box. Everything seemed "the same only
better", but it was not. Even their favourite records
sounded different. His body was still lean and fit and

marvellous to her, but the patterns they made together were different. The seasons had changed and he had not lived them with her.

He drove her home in his cosy little car as he had always done, but when he drew up at the accustomed place, she could not say goodbye.

"Drive to the park," she said. "I can't go home just yet."

They parked by the lake, and watched the deepening dark. The birds and all manner of water fowl settled for the night.

"You've got to tell him, you know," said Zack. "If you're coming to Japan."

"I know I have," said Sarah. "But give me time. You've only just come back." She sniffed the skin of his face and neck like an animal seeking reassurance.

"Better to do it now," said Zack.

She buried her face in his shoulder, but it was hard, sinewy.

"If you say so," she said.

She knew as soon as she turned the key in the lock there was something wrong. It wasn't just the unusual silence, the lack of voices or music, or cigar smoke: it was palpable, an air of misery and defeat that made her pause for a moment before opening the living room door, afraid, and cold with that fear, of what she might find inside.

Adam was sitting in one corner of the sofa looking pale and tense, an empty brandy glass beside him.

My God, she thought. *He knows. He's found out. He's found out at last.* So strong was her relief, she trembled as she crossed the room towards him and dropped to her knees, taking his hands in hers, noticing their coldness.

"What is it, darling? What's the matter?"

His gaze was fixed beyond her at a point above her head, distant as ever.

"They don't want to renew my contract."

"They don't want to—but that's incredible! You've just had the biggest success you've ever had!"

"*You* call it success. *They* call it over-exposure."

"What the hell does that mean?" She sprang to her feet and strode about the room. "They're jealous, of course. You know they are. They don't like you doing New York as well."

"Spare me your theories. They don't want me any more. That's that."

"You've got too big for them. But they'll come round, you'll see. They need you, don't you see? You're the best they've got."

"Don't give me that phoney optimism of yours. That's *all* I need. Let's get out of here. Come on."

Side by side in the cinema dark we see them, coldly holding hands, each playing their own private sound track to the images on the screen. As always.

"I can't tell him now," said Sarah.

"There'll always be a 'now'," said Zack. "If you're really coming, you've got to decide."

"I've decided," yelled Sarah. "There's nothing *to*

decide. How can you keep on nagging me like that? Don't you believe me? I just can't tell him yet."

"There isn't *that* much time," said Zack mildly. "Arrangements to be made. All sorts of things. I haven't told Elizabeth yet, you know. I don't think she'd want to come, she's not all that keen on travelling any more. But if you don't come, Sarah, I must ask her."

"What will she do if she doesn't go with you?" Sarah enquired.

"Oh, she'll stay at 'Fosters', you know. Garden, make preserves, all her usual things. She's very self-contained. And then the children do show up from time to time and they need to know that someone's always there. It's still a home for them, especially in the vac. They bring friends, and the house is full . . ."

"You see how it is," said Sarah. "You can come back —from Japan, I mean—or anywhere else for that matter, and go straight home. Back to the same cosy set-up. No questions asked. But me? If I tell Adam, I can never go back to him. My life would be built entirely around yours. And Adam's life may just conceivably be ruined. Then there's the tiny question of my job. You know what things are like, especially in the media: if you go away for a year you can be quite forgotten. It may seem a silly job to you, but it matters a lot to me. Working is my independence."

"It's simple," said Zack. "A question of priorities. You care more for your trendy life-style than you do for me."

"Oh God, that's so unfair. Everyone wants love *and*

independence. Hardly anyone gets it. You have, and I have. We're lucky. And you're asking me to give mine up."

"Look here," said Zack angrily. "I'm not forcing you to come. You *wanted* to come. Remember?"

After he dropped her, she walked round the square twice making speeches to herself: Everybody needs love and work. How have we managed to polarize our needs until love equals woman and work equals man as if they were truly South and North? And men and women, those mixed elements, longing to lie in one another's arms, can only pass each other endlessly, like the proverbial ships in the night. How can we ever reconcile our lives while men, those Northerners, are taught love is a weakness, an indulgence that interferes with work, and women, so often (even now) denied the right to work, live life for love alone?

4

Paul Blake telephoned Sarah at her office and asked if she would meet him for a drink. He wanted to talk to her, he said. Sarah wondered if he was worried about Linda, who hadn't seemed very well last time they had all met. Though drinks after work always meant missing her sacred hour with Zack, she agreed to meet Paul in the bar of an hotel she liked for its old fashioned air and its quiet.

He was sitting there swigging his Campari-soda, looking glossy and out of place in his trendy gear, every costly item of which vied for attention. Having just landed one of those "prestige" advertising campaigns in which actors are mentioned repeatedly by their own name while being filmed and photographed sampling the "product", he was feeling even more pleased with himself than usual. In addition to the habitual opulent-actor look, Sarah noticed that he had now taken on that special advertising glossiness, that overfed ripeness of the skin around the cheeks and eyes by which we recognise contemporary Lunching Man.

"You're such a chameleon," she said, while he ordered her drink and stared intently at her over the rim of his.

"This has got to stop. It's gone on long enough," he announced, his eyes tracking her legs as far as they could with practised lechery.

"What are you talking about?" asked Sarah.

"You and me, baby. I'm talking about you and me."

"Paul—have you gone mad?"

He began to get annoyed. "My God, you're uptight, Sarah. Let me tell you, the dolly birds, eighteen, nineteen years old, with knockers out to here"—his hands described arcs from his chest—"the long blonde hair, the mini skirts. I can have them all. But I don't want them. I want you. I always have. I just fancy you, that's all."

"Well, thanks very much. I mean, that's very flattering. But Paul . . ."

"You don't fancy *me*? Is that the problem? All these years I thought . . ."

His face was the face now of the Paul she used to know: vulnerable, young, uncertain; the Paul she remembered looking scared to death when he found he'd got Linda pregnant. They were on the dole at the time (he was "resting" between jobs) and they lived in a room above a truss shop. If only she could say: Yes, Paul, that's right. I'm very fond of you, you know I am. But, no, I don't fancy you. That's that. Instead, the coward in her babbled reassuringly:

"You're smashing, Paul. You know you are. But—what about Linda?"

"Don't give me *that*," snapped Paul. "Every girl says that." He mimicked a female voice: "I couldn't hurt your wife."

"For Chrissake, Paul, she's my friend . . ."

"And you're the one who always says that that's what friends are for—would you rather we slept with our enemies? Dear Sarah, Linda's away tonight, and what I propose to do is take you home, undress you and lay you on the sofa in the living room. And I know just what I'm going to do to you." He whispered in her ear.

"Oh, Paul," she said. "I like you. I'm not going to bed with you. I want you to take me home."

His car was like a rather tasteful brothel. She sank into the low soft-textured seat, seductive music (Getz/Gilberto) played, they glided forward with a purr of power. Smells of leather, cigars and breathy alcohol invaded her disturbingly. She would have liked to weep. Instead, she forced herself to say:

"They wouldn't do it to us, you know. They're *good*. And I know what you'd do if Linda was unfaithful. At least I think I do. You'd mind, wouldn't you?"

"You bet I would," said Paul. "I'd beat her black and blue. She wouldn't do it, you know. Not to *me*. The thing is," he said, kindly, "she doesn't fancy other men. She only fancies me. Now look," he said, "if it's Adam, and you've never been unfaithful, I understand the point. But if you decide to start, then start with me." He patted her on the knee and dropped her at the corner of her square. She looked around her guiltily as they stopped in case she had been seen. It seemed to her that she had been unfaithful in some new, degrading way.

She went to a telephone box and dialled Zack's number. It rang and rang (familiar tone) but he didn't answer.

Once more she walked around the square before going home. Well, it had happened at last: he'd succumbed to one of his adoring students. And she had only herself to blame. How could she expect him to believe she loved him when she wouldn't live with him, wouldn't follow him across the world? Oh God. She who had never been able to make any trivial decision: blue shoes or red shoes, she had to have them both. To be faced with this.

But people who left their husbands and went off with their lovers did so because they had stopped loving their husbands, hadn't they? One love had ended when another began. This was something Sarah had never understood. For her it had never been like that, even with friendship. Once involved at depth, you became part of the other's daily life, a necessary part, a need. In her experience, new loves were added to the old and the heart expanded gratefully. Who first set a limit on the capacity of hearts, or saw emotion as a well which could run dry, a poor and finite thing? Who taught us to describe our love as if it were a lake, circumference definite, instead of like all oceans, part of one another, flowing into one another ceaselessly?

When she eventually went up to the flat she found Adam with his old friend and colleague Kenneth. They were working on an idea for a new programme which was to put Adam back at the top of British television. Kenneth, a bachelor who lived alone and had counted their place as his second home for many years, kissed Sarah with all the warmth he reserved for women who were safely married to his friends.

"This is just up your street, my love. We need your help with this. Non-communication between husbands and wives."

"Any wife to any husband?"

"You see?" he said to Adam triumphantly. "She's got the title already."

"Can we have supper, please," said Adam.

When she came back bearing food and wine they were discussing the kind of dreary wifely conversation that made non-communication inevitable: "You can't blame a bloke for clamming up when all he hears is washing machines and floor polish and what the baby said today."

"That's not fair," said Sarah, as she spread out cutlery and dishes. "This man you're talking about . . . when he first married, he probably wanted his wife to be dependent on him for everything. He didn't realise that that meant for interest, too. He's become her window on the world. She wants *him* to talk to *her*. You'd be surprised how quickly the world can be confined to nappies and floor polish, and people need to talk about the things they do each day."

"That's just the kind of woman I can't stand," said Adam, his mouth full. "Totally dependent. No life of her own."

"They go to pieces if you have to go away for a few days and leave them on their own," said Kenneth, wisely. "I know the type."

"I could never marry a woman like that," said Adam smugly, pouring wine.

"Oh, neither could I," said Kenneth.

Sarah left them to make the coffee and when she returned they were gossiping like two old dears.

"Can you blame her for running off," said Adam maliciously. "I mean he never took any notice of her when she was there."

"Never spoke to her at all," echoed Kenneth.

The doorbell rang loudly and they looked at one another, startled for a moment.

"Oh, my God," said Sarah. "I forgot. I invited my parents round for coffee. Can you stand it, Ken?"

"*He* can, if *I* can," said Adam sulkily. He grimaced at Kenneth and they moved together imperceptibly, like boys ganging up for an impending schoolroom battle.

Sarah opened the door and Paul and Linda Blake walked in.

One hand on Sarah's shoulder, one on his wife's, Paul moved jauntily into the sitting room, clapped both the men there on their backs, sat down and lit a small cigar.

"We went out for a meal," he was telling Adam, "and Linda felt she needed cheering up, so where better? Where better? And how are you, my lovely Sarah?"

My lovely Sarah, who you left less than an hour ago. My lovely Sarah who you planned to seduce tonight on your lonely sofa because your wife was away . . .

"I'm fine, thank you," said Sarah, levelly, "but I feel you ought to know my parents are coming round."

At once Paul relaxed into the cushions of his chair, becoming the man most mothers love to meet. When he spoke again his voice was rough and warm with the homely accents of his northern youth.

"We don't mind that, do we, our Linda? Parents like me. You'll see. Linda's mum always fancied me. On the quiet."

"She said you were oversexed," said Linda.

"Because of me ears."

"What's wrong with your ears?" asked Kenneth, fascinated.

"Large lobes," said Paul with satisfaction. "Wanta look?"

Sarah glanced at Adam for strength but he was busy pouring drinks and didn't see. Kenneth moved to investigate Paul's ears. The doorbell rang again.

Later, Sarah's father said:

"We advertised, you see. We wanted someone who would appreciate it. Someone who'd look after it. We lived with it all our married life. Thirty-six years, that bedroom suite. Solid, you know. Walnut outside, mahogany lined . . ."

"They don't make them like that any more," said Paul, his hand shaping the curves of an imaginary wardrobe in the air.

"I needed a change," said Sarah's mother in her high, clear voice. "I wanted something completely different. I said to your father, if I don't change that room now, I never will, it will be too late. I'll get old and that furniture will be the same and I'll always regret not changing it."

"There was one young woman did appreciate it," Sarah's father said to Paul. "Stroked the wood, she did. Inside and out."

"I should get her telephone number if I were you," said Paul. "You could go round and see if she was looking after it."

"*She* was one who would appreciate what she's got," said the old man quietly.

Sarah hovered in the bedroom over the telephone, wondering if she dared call Zack. She lifted the receiver and listened to the burr of the dialling tone. But the extension was in the hall by the living room door and could easily be picked up. Or she might be overheard. She dared not risk it.

Later that night when she couldn't get to sleep, she crept out of bed and crouched silent over the instrument in the dark hall, daring herself to call. But the noise of the dialling tone in the silent house seemed louder than her fears and she replaced the receiver hurriedly and went back to bed, where Adam, who was snoring evenly, grunted and moved over automatically to his side.

For a long time Sarah lay listening to his breathing, and it seemed to her strangely moving, this little sound of life in the enveloping darkness. This particular life. She felt glad she was listening to him, as if she were acknowledging his sleep, affirming that he lived. So many people lie all night breathing in empty rooms, alone.

That night, Sarah, who never dreamed, or never remembered dreams, dreamed she had lost her handbag in a foreign country and had somehow to find her way home without contacts or identity, keys, or a working knowledge of the language. She dialled half-remembered telephone numbers on strangely shaped telephones and was obliged to listen to endless ringing in empty rooms. No one answered her.

When she awoke she knew with certainty that she was pregnant. She had no clear idea of how long she had known, or of exactly which sign or portent had given her this awareness, but the knowledge spread through her body like a warm tide, relaxing her. She put her hands flat on her stomach though there was nothing at all to feel; even her waist seemed exactly the same. But she continued to move her hands slowly over her body, as if it were new.

She had the feeling that some infallible fortune teller had told her she was certain to live happily ever after: it was as if she had seen into the future and knew there would be nothing to worry about ever again. In the same instant of awareness, she had also known that the child was the child of her one carefree afternoon, the only time she had been unfaithful to her husbands. This irony in itself would have convinced her, had she needed convincing. What do you think of that? she asked herself, but found she had no interest in the answer. It didn't seem to matter. She lay in warm mindlessness for a bit, then rolled over so she could tell Adam the news, but he was gone. Breakfast with some American tycoon, she remembered.

She got out of bed and brushed her hair, peering at herself in the glass. She didn't look any different. Was there a slight blueness round the eyes, or had that been there before? It was hard to tell. She made herself tea with toast and honey and took the tray back to bed where she sat fatly propped up with pillows, pretending to read.

5

Dear Doctor X:

I love Z but I'm married to A and I can't seem to leave him.

Why can't you leave him?

Because he's down on his luck.

And before he was down on his luck?

Because he's built a system. I'm one of the foundation stones.

Are you glorifying his dependency on you? Would he— or his system—really collapse without you?

I'd like to think they wouldn't. But I'm afraid they would.

And you can't take that risk?

No, I can't. All the evidence points to collapse.

You still love him.

I suppose I do.

Dear Doctor Y:

I love Z but I'm married to A and I love him too. What shall I do?

Perhaps neither of these gentlemen are right for you. Possibly that is why you think you love them both. You should leave them both and find a third who will satisfy all your needs. (My telephone number is . . .)

Dear Doctor Z:

For a long time now I have loved two men simultaneously and it seems that I cannot be happy unless they both love me. But now I am pregnant and I fear the practical difficulties which will arise when I have the baby . . .

This duality suggests that you cannot be happy with either of these two men. Perhaps you should take your child and go off with another woman. (My telephone number is . . .)

The girls in the office were talking to Miles about a programme they had seen on television the night before about lesbians.

"I thought it was rather ordinary," said Miles.

"Disappointed, were you?"

"Well, there wasn't anything special about any of those people, was there? I mean they seemed just like anybody else. Rather a dreary bunch of females."

"He means they weren't much like those glamorous creatures he drools at in his sexy magazines; the ones who lick each other's tits for his delight."

"Some of them seemed a bit larger than life."

"Enormous," said Miles. "You'd be like an asparagus waving about in the Albert Hall."

"I can see what they mean about sex with other women," said a secretary. "I mean, another woman would know exactly what you wanted, wouldn't she?"

"And it is true," said another. "Women can go on and on. Men always come to a stop."

"That's ridiculous," Miles exploded, outraged. "Just because you're all married to insensitive brutes doesn't mean men can't know exactly what turns a woman on."

The girls turned on him: "You mean we haven't tried you," they said, in chorus.

Sarah went down to the pub with Miles and they discussed the series. It was shaping up nicely now, and Sarah's interviewing work was almost at an end. "There are just two or three more interviews I'd like to do," she told him, "and then we can call it quits. There's so much material now, it's drawing the conclusions that's going to be the problem."

"I'm telling you, girl," said Miles, "this series is going to be a knockout. We might even put the circulation up by two or three. Mind you, I always knew it. I never wavered." He paused, awaiting her congratulations.

She was rather later than usual arriving at Zack's. On the doorstep of the apartment block, a slim, raincoated figure exuding an aura of drink and guilt waited by the bell.

"I'll let you in," said Sarah, fumbling for her key.

Suddenly, a weary female voice complained loudly through the answerphone: "Oh, you've arrived, have you?" it said. "About time! I'd given you up."

The stranger shot Sarah a rueful look. The disembodied voice, gravelly with reproach, hung in the air between them.

They went up together in the lift, a powerful smell of *Calandre* left by the last occupant mingling with the whiffs of tobacco and alcohol coming from the man. He had been to a party. He leaned back against one wall of the lift and surveyed Sarah, who leaned against the other. Both drunk, both late, both guilty. He smiled at her, and she smiled back. Complicity.

"I like your . . . er, hair," he said, in a lazy drawl, making a slow gesture with his hands, an arc, a waterfall. "It's . . ." —smile crinkling in effort—"nice."

His voice was resonant with worldliness, and the silly word somehow held all the possibilities, even tenderness and regret. A sexy American! What next?

"Thank you," she smiled. The lift stopped. He turned up his collar as he left her, as if he were going out in the cold again. She pictured the greeting he had in store from gravel-voice. Would he silence her with kissing? Would he argue: Okay, I'm late, but I'm here now, so shut up, before dragging her off to bed? Perhaps he'd be booted out: it's no good coming in late and making excuses. You've ruined my evening; you can go.

Zack was not there when she got to the flat and she sat in the darkness waiting. Perhaps I will never see him again, she thought. Perhaps he's left me for good. Good? It's all my own fault, of course. What did I give him, what did he ever gain from me? I messed up his life, that's all. She jumped when she heard the key in the lock and waited for the blonde giggle she felt sure would follow him.

"Sarah," he said. He leaned over the chair and kissed her on the mouth. It seemed there was no one with him.

"Where have you been?" Did it sound as sullen, as panicky as it felt?

"Oh, to 'Fosters', darling. I tried to let you know but I couldn't get hold of you, and I didn't like to leave a message."

He began to switch on lamps. "What's wrong? You look pale," he said.

"Nothing. I'm pregnant."

"Good Lord." He knelt in front of her low armchair and searched her face intently.

"Darling, I'm happy for you." He took her hands in his and kissed the fingertips, then rested his head gently on her stomach. Like a commercial, she thought.

"Do you feel any different?" he asked.

"No," said Sarah. "Aren't you going to ask me if it's yours?"

He pulled his head away and looked at her: a long and level look. "No," he said. "No. I don't want to know it's mine. Unless I can take full responsibility."

They sat looking at one another for a while.

"What does that mean?" she asked him. "Acknowledging the child? Leaving Adam. Coming to Japan. Living together when we get back?"

Silence. He had put his head back on her stomach again, and seemed to be asleep. She felt deserted. Yet the weight of his head on her stomach was comforting: she almost fell asleep herself.

She saw herself suddenly at the end of a dark room being wrapped in red blankets by two giant firemen. She was ten years old and had been burned when a chip pan had gone up in flames: so much for her attempts to prepare a proper grown-up supper for her father. Later, her father came home, passing two fire engines at the gate, and saw his daughter being swaddled in scarlet by the firemen. The look on his face told her everything she had ever wanted to know about her father: her heart moved painfully then and now as she recalled that stricken look. But she could not forgive him: he had not been there when it had happened.

"You won't be here when it happens," she said suddenly to Zack. "I'll need you. I'll be afraid. And you won't be there." They were both awake now, and Zack was angry.

"Then come with me, you idiot," he said.

"What, and have the baby in Japan?"

"Good God, it's not Timbuctoo, you know. Japan is a modern industrialized society. Babies are born there every day—rather too many of them, actually. Hospitals exist. Honestly, Sarah, I thought you had more guts. Do you think I wouldn't look after you, or something?" They glared at one another, warily.

"Or is it the reverse?" said Zack. "That's it! You don't want to be dependent on me, do you? You and your careful system of checks and balances."

"You'd love it, of course," said Sarah bitterly. "I can see it all. Carefree professor, no family ties, have-brain-will-travel, followed over hill and dale by forlorn female carrying papoose. But you'd be kind to us: you'd throw us scraps of your raw fish and the dregs of last night's *saké*. They've a healthy attitude to women and children in Japan, or hadn't you noticed?"

"You won't get beaten unless you fail to leave the room silently, backwards and on your knees," said Zack.

They both laughed, and the tension snapped.

"Or remember to use the bathwater *after* me." They hugged each other. "I can't remember the last time I fucked a pregnant lady," he said.

"As you roll your *tatami*, so you must lie on it," said Sarah.

"Or something," mumbled Zack.

6

Sarah had collaborated with Adam and Kenneth on the treatment of the idea for the new programme *Any Wife to Any Husband,* and Adam had gone off to Bavaria to get a European co-production deal. With this in his pocket, and the American tie-up ensured, he could say "up yours" to the company which had fired him.

There had been a ghastly moment a few days back when he'd come in beaming all over, swung Sarah off her feet and told her: "We're going to New York."

"How long for?" she'd asked him, unable to hide her dismay.

"How should I know?" was the jaunty reply. "For ever, I should think. It's where I'm loved. That oil tycoon promised me millions of dollars."

New York with Adam and the baby; no domestic help; no jobs for English journalists; endless cocktail parties and steely skyscrapers; complete dependency; coffee mornings with other captive wives; compulsory psychoanalysis. New York, where the most popular triangular relationship was man, wife and psychiatrist.

Fortunately for Sarah, friends and admirers warned Adam that his success in the States depended on his being British, on his arriving fresh from England every week bearing new titbits of gossip and information. The American public liked him for his transatlantic "class", for his European charm. The crisis passed.

"I've got something to tell you," she sang out now as she opened the door and saw his suitcases bearing Bavarian stickers in the hall.

"Not as exciting as what I've got to tell you. We've got the deal! You want to see?" He pulled out a signed contract all in Gothic script and waved it at her. "We're in business again! We can eat! What's for supper?"

"This child's upstaged by television at an early age," she muttered, moving towards the kitchen, but Adam didn't hear.

Later, when she'd fed him and he'd almost gone to sleep, she tried again to tell him about the baby, and he seemed to hear her. At any rate he looked at her solemnly. "Good thing it didn't happen last week, my girl. We couldn't have afforded it, y'know."

Mel, Mel, where are you now that I need you? You'll have to come back now so we can share the baby. It's your Godchild, you silly twit. That's it: we'll bring it up together. Our baby, inculcated from the beginning with all the wrong ideas. It had better be a girl . . .

Mel's letters, of late, had been rambling dissertations on *A Doll's House*, the two-party system, the Celtic twilight; they contained nothing as practical as a telephone number or the address of her ever-changing digs. Nevertheless, Sarah tried to telephone her, using a mysteriously long string of numbers she'd looked up. The first time there was no answer, and the second she got a scornful female voice which told her there was no one there at the moment, suggested she try the Residents Hall, then rang off without giving her the number.

Who was it who said work is the true salvation? I think it was me. She prepared for another interview.

> He felt he couldn't hold me, you see. I was getting so successful and he must have felt I was outgrowing him as a person. So he started tying me up and then he started using objects to do it with—oh, candles and things like that—and in the end I felt like an object myself: a thing, whose reactions he watched in a horrid way while he himself stayed cool. Funny, really, when our sex life had always been one of the best things about our marriage. And him having had a vocation—oh, yes, he'd wanted to be a priest, probably still does for all I know.

Miles had been interviewing secretaries all day and was even now comparing the statistics of the more nubile candidates in the privacy of his inner office. As Sarah sat at her desk and began to type, Irene, the woman's page editor, came over.

"You should have been here today," she told Sarah, perching her square behind on a nearby desk, and lighting herself a cigarette. "A regular beauty contest. Everything but the swimsuit parade. I can't wait to see Miss World."

"What do you expect?" said Sarah, passing Irene a

page of Situations Vacant ads with one ad circled in purple ink. GIRL FRIDAY FOR FEATURES EDITOR. Unshockable. Unflappable. Experienced. Only girls of willing disposition need apply.

Irene inhaled deeply and blew smoke from her nostrils in an angry snort. "If it got about that that was for this paper, all my campaigns for the status of secretaries, our committee for better conditions for women at work, our lobby for office crèches, could be sent up rotten. All we need is a spy inside this place for *Private Eye*."

"Just another of life's little balancing acts," said Sarah, as the door burst open and a red-faced Miles puffed in.

"My God," he said, "women are absolutely mad. That last one must have been ten months pregnant, at least. What she wants a job for, I can't imagine. Should have thought she'd got one that'll keep her busy for years."

"Miles," said Irene, patiently, wrinkling her eyes through smoke, "do you ever read the woman's page?"

"Discrimination," said Miles. "Segregation."

"Discrimination's what you're doing now," said Sarah. "You want someone to start in three months time, don't you? A girl like that has obviously got plans to be ready for work again after the baby."

"And what'll she do with the brat?" Miles spat. "Bring it in in a basket and have it mewling and puking over the office carpet?"

"Mind you, missing the first months of your baby's development for fulfilling work as Miles' secretary does seem a bit strong," said Irene.

"How would you know?" asked Miles.

Sarah winced.

"It was different in my day!" replied Irene calmly. "A career girl wasn't even married, let alone pregnant. The Bad Old Days," she added wistfully.

"What if you'd made her pregnant yourself?" Sarah asked Miles.

"Who? That girl? Nice of you—but I never set eyes on her before!"

"No, silly. If you made your secretary pregnant, would you let her go on working for you?"

"I'd have to sack her, wouldn't I? I couldn't let her be seen. I've got *some* morals. I never let my wife work after we had our brood, either."

"Did she want to?"

"Fucking women's union round here tonight. I suppose you'd like me to be queer, so I could employ a dishy little boy as secretary."

"An idea for our next series," said Sarah suddenly. "An investigation into working mothers. *How* they do it. *Why* they do it."

"Good," nodded Irene.

"That should lose what remains of the circulation," said Miles.

"And to think I was about to tell him about me," Sarah muttered as he left.

"What, dear?" said Irene absently.

"Oh, nothing," said Sarah.

Beep . . . Beep . . . sound of coins clonking into a telephone box. "Mel!" said Sarah. "Oh, I'm so glad. I've got something marvellous to . . ."

Beep . . . Beep . . . the line went dead. When it rang again a voice said, "Wales. Will you pay for the call?"

"Yes, *Yes*," said Sarah. "Mel! Where have you been? Where *are* you? I've tried . . ."

Hospital: the word dropped coldly into her ear and stopped her joyful flow. "Hospital?"

"You heard," said Mel gruffly. "Some little woman's trouble. No, not my tubes again. I've had a miscarriage."

There was a pause for some strangled, gulping noises, then the familiar voice, shaky but in control, went on: "That's what it's called. Miscarriage. It sounds Victorian, doesn't it? I do assure you, it is not."

"Oh, Mel!" (Who, what, when?) "How long?" asked Sarah.

"Two months; well, actually, nine weeks. But it was *there.*"

"Shall I come up?"

The sound of Mel's crying travelled like pain along the line.

"Not now. It's over. I'm all right, *I*'ll live."

"I'll come tonight."

"No," said Mel. "No point. They're keeping me in here for another week. There's nothing you can do. Besides, I feel better now I've told you. Honestly."

Sarah got the name of the hospital from her, and the number.

"Promise you'll ring again tomorrow night? Reverse the charges, we can have longer, then. You'll feel better tomorrow, you'll see."

"I feel better already. I told you. Forgive me."

Forgive? Oh, Mel.

Sarah sat shivering in the dark hugging her own small swelling middle. What was that all about? And who, what, when? In the few months that Mel had been in Wales a whole new daylight dream had been born in her again; her eternal quest for the Holy Grail of happiness once more embarked upon. This time the dream must have been that she would have a baby—any baby—and she and the child would be happy, alone, together forever. She must have thought she would never need men again, nor any of the baffling complications of the outside world. The secret of human life so safely within herself had seemed All Human Life, her hopes for it, all Hope. Oh, Mel. All your eggs in one basket. And now, all bled away. Bleached. Beached. Stranded. Sarah rocked herself back and forth, tears falling on the hands she clasped across her belly. "Do you hear me, in there, infant?" she said angrily. "I won't make *you* 'all my happiness' I promise. There are burdens enough in store for you, God knows."

Zack was correcting the proofs of his book when Sarah let herself in to the flat next evening. He was bent over his desk, his back to the room, but the tension evident in every line of his shoulders and head communicated itself to her before she was inside the door. She put her hands on his neck and massaged that eloquent knob at the top of the spine. "What's wrong? Are you re-writing it all again?"

"It's shit," said Zack wearily, pushing her hands away and lighting a cigarette. A half-smoked cigarette smouldered already in an ashtray full of butts.

"Shit, it is not," said Sarah. "Go and lie down. You need a break. I'll get you a Scotch. Or would you like some tea?"

"It's a lousy book. Shoddy. Already out of date," said Zack. But he went to the sofa, kicked off his shoes, lay down, while she fetched him his drink.

"And don't start with your encouraging noises, lady. I know when something I've done's no good. Coming here like some latter-day Florence Nightingale dispensing literary lampshine."

"Pollyanna," said Sarah. "Cheers."

"That's right. Cheers. Mixing drinks, dispensing food. A little love, a little sex. A little cheer. Cheers us old academics up all right, keeps us going, don't y'know."

He gulped his whisky: "Bring the bottle over. I need some more."

For the first time that evening he looked directly at her, and she saw that the well-assembled architecture of his face was trembling on the point of collapse, of ruin. "What's wrong with you, Zack?"

"Come here!" he demanded, and, holding her, drove his head painfully into the space between her breasts. After a minute or so, he thrust her away from him and regarded her with a composure so rigid she knew it for a warning.

"I've something to tell you," he said.

Sarah sat down.

"I told Elizabeth about Japan. She wants to come with me." Pause. "The awful thing is, she broke down. I mean, she cried." The rigid new mask of his face twitched in embarrassment.

"It seems that—all this time—she hasn't been happy, after all. I've thought she was so contented, I thought it suited her, me being here, her being at 'Fosters'. She always seemed so self-contained; her country husbandry, her gardening, her books. I thought . . . Do you know, she said she'd been lonely?"

Sarah stared at the untouched whisky in her glass. No wonder they called it liquid amber. It was beautiful. Clear. Like the eyes of a jungle cat who has never seen man. Like a tiger.

"Did she know about us?"

"Well, no. Not exactly. I mean, she obviously guessed something. She must know I've had girls. Even, perhaps, that I've been involved. But something like this, as important as this . . ." he looked at her lamely over the rim of his glass, gulped, gestured. "She's no idea," he said finally.

"But—she is—suspicious, I suppose. In a general way. And it's making her unhappy."

He closed his eyes as if they hurt. "Oh, Sarah, how can I have been so wrong about my wife? The woman I lived with all those years. And if I could be so wrong—so insensitive to her, what else have I misunderstood, I wonder?

"The thing is, you see, it has made me feel dreadfully guilty. I never felt guilty before at all. Like you with Adam, I never felt I was taking anything away from Elizabeth. Anything she wanted, or noticed the absence of, that is." He poured himself another drink. "Now it seems what little she does suspect—or know—upsets her very much. She's not demonstrative, you know, Elizabeth.

Never was. And so I never really thought it mattered to her, my not being around, not being about the house—all that. I blame myself so much now for not noticing her mood, not picking up vibes, as the kids say. I suppose I didn't want to notice. She thinks if we go away together we can make . . ."

"A new start."

Sarah finished the well-worn phrase for him, sensing from the dread she could feel building up inside her, he was asking her to finish so much more. Well, she could not. There was a limit even to *her* strength, *her* willingness to please. Let him perform the grisly deed himself. She was filling nicely with baby, but her insides felt hollow as a gong. Time, distance, a new start, an old ending—all meaningless to the heart. We cannot easily unlearn our loves.

7

Adam seemed to feel secure enough now about the new series to buy a new motor and suggest they take a holiday.

"Do you the world of good," he told Sarah. "Give you a bit of a break before maternity sets in."

The bright new symbol of his reborn confidence—a red Maserati—stood waiting to be run in.

"I could do with a rest," agreed Sarah.

So they took a boat to Bilbao, drove to Altamira and back and caught a plane to Madrid.

"Feeling better?" Adam asked her in the Prado, as she endeavoured to stop the floor tilting towards her and concentrate on the black Goyas in a temperature of 100 degrees. Later, they went to Pamplona for the running of the bulls. They were up at five o'clock every morning and stayed up for the dancing at night.

"A change is as good as a rest," Adam assured her.

"Besides, a fiesta is a fiesta is a fiesta, as Miss Stein might so easily have said. Anyway, if we don't stay till the end, you'll miss the fireworks, and I know how much you love fireworks."

He drove the car round and round in the forest below the citadel, showing her turrets and parapets and angles.

Inevitably, they hit a tree. One headlight was shattered, and the wing damaged. Tragedy. It was Sunday, too.

"Nothing is open," he lamented, sitting helplessly in front of the steering wheel, the great powerful red engine silent.

"Hotels have garages," she pointed out.

He went off to see it if were true.

She sat by the car on a green bank, admiring the newly acquired tan of her legs against the eggshell blue of her linen dress. The loudest sounds were the rasping of cicadas and the running of a brook as it cascaded across stones to join the moat at the bottom of the hill. Butter-flies flew everywhere. She chewed grass and rested. She was happy.

Eventually, Adam returned with a red-faced mechanic in blue overalls, who lowered his head when he saw the car and went for it as if it were a bull in the ring. Adam stood silently as the man wrestled with the metal bulk of the heavy engine. Slowly, by sheer brute force, his neck getting ever redder, the mechanic shifted the enormous bonnet, disengaging wood from metal. A sizeable chunk had been taken from the trunk of the tree.

Listening to Adam thanking the man and asking what he wanted in payment, Sarah indulged in a fantasy:

"I want her—" said the mechanic, pointing at Sarah.

Adam registered surprise, then got into his motor,

drove it a few yards and parked with his back to Sarah and the man. The man grabbed Sarah by the arm and pulled her down the hill to where the brook she had heard flowed under scrub and bushes. He pushed her to the ground and took off her knickers, opened his dungarees and took out his cock, which was large and even redder than his neck. Sarah noted with pleasure how clean it looked.

Without fuss, he pushed himself into her and started to thrust. Pine needles pressed into her bottom and the rhythmic grunts of the mechanic joined the sounds of the brook and the cicadas. Presently, a smell of sweat and semen mixed strongly with the smell of pine, crushed herbs and grass. When the mechanic had finished, he handed Sarah her knickers, buttoned himself up and walked up the hill again, nodding to Adam as he passed the car. Sarah washed in the stream, dried herself, and followed.

"No serious damage," said Adam, as she joined him in the car. "I think we can go on, don't you?"

They drove across an amazing desert, hatted, scarved and goggled against the bitter dust like early motorists. Sand-coloured cities rose up from the sand in front of them like mirages. After Zaragoza they discovered Lérida. The cool galleries and dusty dignity of the place soothed the rash which had appeared on her arms and calmed the twinges in her intestines. They ate marvellously. "I shall love Spain forever, if I survive," said Sarah.

"That's how the Spaniards feel," said Adam.

And Zack? Will I love him forever, too? And miss him forever?

Zack, Zack, she whispered in the dark corners of baroque churches, where blank-faced madonnas regarded her, unperturbed. She lit guttering candles on altars where she knew they would burn slowly through the night. The thought comforted her. She wondered why.

Night after night she wondered why she had not said all the things to him she now said sleeplessly to her unyielding Spanish pillow: a catechism, a rosary, a series of spells as one-way as any prayers:

What if he doesn't love me any more?

But he does, I know he does!

Perhaps he'll forget you. A year's a long time.

Nonsense! What's a year?

Twelve months, 365 days—and nights—that's a year.

A trivial year. A mere sixth of our time together.

It's a sickness. You'll get over it. You won't care any more.

I'll always care.

Don't you want to get over it?

I can't, I've tried.

This must stop. It's obsessive. Don't think about him all the time.

But I miss him.

Forget him.

I love him.

How do you know?

I know. And I'll always love him.

Whatever happens?

Whatever happens.
This must stop. Try harder.
I'm trying.
Try harder.
I can't. I've tried.

Even in the unshadowed daylight, she carried images of death with her across the Iberian continent. Wild generalisations are sometimes true—perhaps the Spanish do have a national death wish, after all. Grimaces from the black Goyas followed her into the narrow streets: blood from gory baroque crucifixes congealed in her mind. The harsh sounds of flamenco singing were death-rattle, lament, anguished ritual wail: the heart had been plucked out of Spain and her sons mourned. Her daughters, of course, danced nightly at her funeral. Survivors of the civil war, men who had been mutilated by their brothers using old tin cans as weapons, unwound their wounds for a peseta, and six black bulls, all brave and beautiful, sank to their knees each week as the sword plunged accurately to its mark.

It was no surprise to Sarah when, a week or so after their return to London, Adam's mother telephoned, her voice sounding strained and far away. "I think you'd better come," she said. "Dad's ill."

"Adam's away again," said Sarah. "I'll be there in an hour."

Does death come to these neat, efficient suburbs, too? This is not Spain: no violence finds its way down weed-less garden paths or past trim hedges. No poison ivy climbs these walls. Yet even here where chiming door-bells chime synthetic welcome, the panelled door swings open to reveal the pit. It was just a disaster area like any other.

Relics of human comfort lay abandoned on the Persian carpet: a water bottle, a slipper, a walking stick. On a velvet chair in a yellow plastic potty, floated a single turd. On the sofa sat an old man in an old dressing gown, his white patrician head nodding on his breast, his head framed, in Sarah's angle of vision, by the spangled breasts of two bright black chorus girls bouncing and singing on the colour television. Adam's mother, still orderly in her appearance in her cashmeres and tweeds in the midst of this disorder, seemed the most disturbing element of all.

Who would have thought that those elegant hands of hers which rested on the pearls at her throat in the portrait over the piano, which had languished so roman-tically on the piano keys in the days of her courting, which had learned neither to cook nor to sew, would one day plunge into the rectum of her husband and help him produce that single pale turd with the minimum of effort, lest he strain his heart? Now that turd reproached her from the velvet chair and Mrs Cornish twisted and kneaded her beautiful hands as she talked. She's "wring-ing her hands", thought Sarah.

Adam's mother moved distractedly through her rooms talking as she went. "The geraniums wouldn't grow this year. And we've had wonderful weather. I knew there was something wrong. My geraniums always grow."

A cylinder of oxygen stood against a wall in the hall.

"We had an emergency while you were in Spain. Then he improved. Now they're coming to take him to hospital. They'll soon be here. It's for the best. He doesn't want to go."

"They'll look after you so much better there than I can, darling," she pleaded. "They have all the equipment—everything."

"You must get better quickly," Sarah said. "This baby's going to need a grandpa."

The old man gazed at Sarah's tummy silently.

I don't want to go into hospital. And you know why. I may never come out again. Never again. But the thought was unspoken, and because of that, seemed almost unthinkable, too.

Two gentle, kindly giants arrived with the ambulance. "Well, sir," they said, assessing the scene with practised eyes, "I expect you'll feel better like this." They wrapped a scarlet blanket round the old man, and, in one swift movement, raised him to his feet. The vivid beauty of the scene disconcerted Sarah. She had expected dignity and pathos, and so could find comfort in them, but these dazzling colours, the scarlet blanket brilliant against the shapely silver head, and the silver startling next to the jaundiced false-tan of his face, caused her to blink and turn her head away.

Dextrously, and in a matter of minutes, they had him comfortably in the ambulance. The two Mrs Cornishes followed behind in the Cornish car. Adam's mother concentrated hard on driving, while Sarah stared unbelieving out of the window. The blank end of the ambulance preceded them like a hearse.

"Such a lovely day," Mrs Cornish repeated. "Such a lovely day."

The ambulance wound along the common and past the parks and across the heath as if to allow the old man a last tour of his favourite spots. All those walks, years, blackberries, dogs. Farewell. All my moods and seasons.

"How can it be such a lovely day," muttered Mrs Cornish.

8

The world grew gradually smaller as her belly grew
bigger, and this seemed perfectly fair: she was absorbed,
like any pregnant woman in an inner world. Zack gone.
Mel gone. Adam more often than not, away. Job almost
finished. What did she care? She grew like the herbs in
her window boxes, flourishing like the green bay tree.
Her geraniums, unlike those of her mother-in-law,
flowered brilliantly that year, and there seemed a mad
kind of logic in it.

When she visited the hospital where the old man lay,
she was conscious that she brought life in all its brutal
radiance to startle and confront the old, the sick, the
dying. Yet she did not feel embarrassed by her intrusion.
Perhaps being pregnant makes you insensitive, she
thought. Perhaps it needs to. Gaily, she discussed the
birth date of her child, its chances with the stars, its
heritage of genes. Placidly, she read the legend on the
white card at the foot of the old man's bed: "Born 1900
——" There was a gap beside it for another date: white
beds, white tombstones. Death must be colourless. Would
he last until the baby's birth? Would he last the year?

Pots of flowers which had outlived the patients they were brought for, sat massed together in the centre of the ward. The dying watched these plants suspiciously.

"Cheerful, aren't they?" remarked the sister, as Sarah left the ward.

"Cheerful," echoed Sarah, beaming at the old men as she passed their beds as if conferring honours.

"I've discovered the secret of cheerfulness," she wrote to Mel. "Don't think. I potter around most of the time now, without a thought in my head. You should try a little of this vegetable life. It's not only good for you— it's pleasant. Cows chewing their cud, are, after all, serene. Cabbages growing in the sun are fat and happy. We don't have to be thinking creatures *all* the time. Has that occurred to you? Unwind. Let yourself go, feel yourself grow. Relax."

It all began with my father, I suppose. Sex and competitiveness. An old story. My sister was prettier than me and my father fancied her more, so I was always knocking myself out to impress him, winning everything in sight from races to exams. But I was never sure he'd noticed. And she was still prettier than me, anyway. And then, when I was fourteen I had a nasty experience. I suppose you could call it rape, really. I couldn't react to sex after that. People may think I'm very sexy—my husband does, for instance—but in fact it wasn't until last year that I had my first orgasm. With my lover—he's someone

```
I've been sleeping with for years. I
just couldn't relax enough before.
Funny, isn't it? All those years of
marriage, two children, lots of affairs—
and only now can I relax into sex, only
now do I learn what it's all about. So
here I am—nice husband, nice kids, good
job, reliable lover, plenty of admira-
tion. I'm just looking for someone to
fall in love with, that's all.
```

"I think we could use this one as the last," Sarah wrote
to Miles across the bottom of the page. "Now I need two
weeks of peace and quiet and I'll have the series written
up."

Lovers like birds flocked towards her as to a warmer
clime, inhabiting her spare-room (soon to be the nursery)
with their brief intensities, arriving at all hours of the
night, departing, mostly, with the dawn. Sometimes a
pair of them would settle on the edge of her bed to preen
themselves in another's eyes before flying off again. With
their arms round one another's necks and their identical
ear-to-ear grins, the man and woman in each couple
seemed to take on likeness from each other until they
became uncannily like twins. Even their giggles were
indistinguishable. Their wine-dark breath mixed strangely
with the odours of cocoa and cold cream which hung
about Sarah's room these days.

```
I'd never get married again. Never.
What would be the point? You'd just be
swapping one domestic set-up for
another. It all comes down to how you
```

like your eggs done for breakfast and
whether you sleep in a hot or cold room.
It's all about habit—marriage—it has to
be—it's for everyday. One marriage is
much the same as another marriage, in
the end, whoever you're married to. But
every love affair is different.

"Now I've finished writing up the series, I think *this*
should be the final interview," Sarah wrote to Miles.
"This one definitely says FADE OUT: THE END. But as it
worked out, she found another somewhere in her research
file which seemed even more appropriate for the final
statement of the series.

You can be lonelier inside a marriage
than any other kind of loneliness: the
people who live by themselves can't know
that feeling of a married person left
alone. Since I was married, I've faced
every single important crisis of my life
alone: I was alone when I had the
babies; when his mother died; when my
mother died. There was that dreadful
time when Pam, my daughter, had
appendicitis and he was away, and I had
to half carry her half drag her to the
hospital: I've never forgotten that
night: she was only eleven but I couldn't
carry her properly by myself: she was
too heavy, or I was too weak . . . They
say you're born alone and you die alone
and it's true. I suppose people think
marriage changes that. I suppose that's
why a lot of them do it. But no
institution on earth can change those
facts. Marriage certainly doesn't . . .

The fact that there were so many endings to a series which seemed to conclude that marriage itself was ending had not escaped her, nor had the fact that she seemed reluctant to write "the end" to the series herself. This was, of course, because now that Miles had noticed her pregnancy, there would be no more work from him, however good the series. She could not expect him to consider her for work again until she could present herself convincingly as a carefree no-strings career girl. Yet this injustice, which would once have worried and angered her, seemed unimportant now. She accepted it as she accepted so much these days: the heaviness of Zack's absence; the sick feeling of disorientation it caused her; Adam's endless comings and goings and his carefully planned details of the nursery, the equipment, the home help they would need. The baby must not on any account be allowed to interfere with him or his carefully evolved life-style. "No excuse for you to become a cabbage," he warned Sarah at frequent intervals, until she thought she must be growing pale green leaves about her ears.

Yet none of this reached her. It seems you must accept the world when you are carrying a baby, for no woman wants to bring a child into a worthless world. And Sarah, as the baby grew inside her and began to kick, felt weighted down by a new conviction: anger and irritation were more than a waste of time, they seemed destructive to such a purposeful and determined growing.

When the pains started she was not prepared for them and for the first few hours in her hospital bed worried mostly about whether there were enough lemons in the fridge and if she had remembered to put the oven on automatic so that the casserole she had left for Adam and Kenneth would be ready for them when they came in that evening. Then she worried about Zack: about where he was now and how he was feeling. It had always been so important for her to know how he felt, to know that he was well, and now she could not know. She could not even visualise him properly outside the context of their flat, their private world. Tears flowed from under her clenched eyelids at the thought of strangers living there among the decorations she had chosen so lovingly for themselves alone. The need to have him with her now, he above all human beings in the world, pressed down on her unbearably. She seemed unable to suppress the knots of grief which tightened in her chest as the contractions tightened in her abdomen. The loss of Zack at this moment seemed the sharpest of all the pains she had to bear. What a ridiculous person I am, she sobbed, always longing for one person when I'm with another, always thinking of one place when I'm in another.

So many nights in the early years of her marriage she had dreamed this moment: the excitement, the fear. Sometimes the dreams had been more like nightmares and her body had undergone unimaginable grotesqueries in an atmosphere of hushed expectancy—but even after these dreams she had woken with a sense of disappointment and inadequacy which had persisted for days.

Now the longed-for experience was upon her and she was not experiencing it: she was not even sure it was real.

Then the pains started in earnest, and there was no time for anything but the pains. She need not have worried: she was forced to concentrate, forced to experience it all.

9

Coming home with the baby in her arms as she had so often dreamed of doing, she was overwhelmed by the colour and soft beauty of the place after the whiteness of the hospital. Had there always been such a seductive air about these rooms, such an enchanting vibrancy of colour? She walked from room to room, hugging him tightly, showing him everything, explaining how the plane trees would become mobiles for him, shaking their leaves through every separate season. She showed him the flowers in the window boxes, and the sunlight dancing on her melon- and honey- and earth-coloured walls. She knew he was much too young to see or appreciate any of these wonders, and the fact disturbed her not at all.

"Oh, we're lucky, we're lucky, we're lucky," she chanted, rocking him as she walked. A feeling of calm, of expectancy satisfied, engulfed her. There would be no empty rooms ever again.

Days, weeks passed. She could not have said what had filled them but she knew they were well filled. Had she believed in contentment, she might have said she was content. The baby evolved into a person called David and if the household revolved around him it seemed to do so without excluding anyone else.

Adam's reactions never ceased to surprise her: at first he took little or no interest in the baby himself, but pronounced readily on all sorts of topics from breast feeding to potty training, laying down the law on everything from fresh air to schooling with the air of someone who has always had a good research team behind him. Then someone suggested that he do a television series on fathers and children, and he came home from the studio full of the idea that modern fathers are deprived of fatherhood by the fashion for mothers-and-babies. Thus did baby David become an integral part of Adam's life.

One of the things Sarah enjoyed most about her life with David was their walks. She would wheel the pram to different parks and to different parts of each park in search of things which might one day amuse him, making up games she'd love to play herself in the hope he might one day like them too. In this way, her London took on yet another new aspect: she saw it now through David's eyes.

One day she had wheeled the pram to one of those small London gardens recovered from an ancient cemetery. An old lady with the kind of plump-cheeked, unlined face worn by the elderly who have not yet begun to live, bore down upon her, swooping and peering into the pram, clucking like a demented duck. "Just like the baby Jesus, isn't he?" She opened a bag full of crusts and started tossing them in the air, while a group of singularly scruffy looking pigeons stood around waiting for the flying crusts to land so they could look them over. "How did I know he was a boy? Well, I've a gift, haven't I? A divine gift. Divination, you know. When he's older he can help me feed the pigeons. Loaves and fishes. Loaves and fishes. I never had a baby. Could have, if I'd wanted. Could have had a dozen. A man called Cook wanted to marry me—imagine it, Mr and Mrs Cook and all the little Cooks—well, after I'd thought of that, I couldn't marry him, could I? Not with a name like that. Mind, I'm happy as the Queen. I have a lovely life. I go home and shut me door and put the kettle on. I put me feet up and have me cuppa tea. She can't be happier than I am in her palace, can she? She can't be more content, over 'er cuppa tea?"

Sarah left her feeding the royal pigeons and pushed the pram towards the rose garden surrounding a small playground. She didn't see Jonathan approach; the tall blond figure standing in front of the pram quite startled her.

"Sarah! How are you? You look lovely. I didn't know you had a baby!" He looked with genuine interest into the pram.

"Easy to tell he's a boy. Smashing little chap, isn't he. About two months old, I'd guess."

Sarah was impressed. "That's clever of you. And almost exact. How did you know?"

"Oh, I like children, y'know. I study them quite a bit. I didn't know you'd got one, though."

"I didn't have. He's new. As a matter of fact, he's yours."

"He's *what*?" Jonathan's face went through all the comical contortions of extreme surprise. Sarah watched it as if she were at the circus.

"Do you know, that was like a firework display and a thunderstorm all rolled into one. You've got an actor's face, Jonathan."

Now Jonathan's face had changed again and seemed to be grinning hugely. He peered into the pram again but David was absorbed in watching his own fingers and took no notice of him at all.

"Well, I must say, you look pleased with yourself," said Sarah.

"I am. But that's my line. You're spoiling the dialogue. I don't know what to say."

"You're the playwright."

"May I walk you home?" asked Jonathan.

So Jonathan walked Sarah and David home and accompanied them up to the nursery and somehow he was still there at bedtime so he helped bath David and put him to bed. Then he took Sarah in his arms behind the nursery door and kissed her well.

"Watch out," said Sarah, "I'm not ready for another one just yet."

"But I'm a family man," said Jonathan.

"Good Lord, what does *that* mean?" said Sarah.

"Relax. I want to see you and the baby regularly."

"A man of many families," she murmured.

About a month after this, Miles came to see Sarah and suggested a new series on Sex and Motherhood. The marriage series had been so successful, he reported grudgingly, that he'd been asked to see if she would contemplate another.

"That is, if you can bear to leave the brat," he said.

David, who never cried, let out a howl.

"He knows I'm not on his side," said Miles.

"Are you on mine?" asked Sarah.

Three months later, when Jonathan's visits had become a delightful once a week routine, when the new programme "Fathers and Babies" was about to be sold to the U.S. and a charming young daily nanny who adored David had decided to come and live in so Sarah could manage better working hours, a letter dropped through the letter box for Sarah marked "Private and Confidential". It bore Japanese stamps.

"Only three months more to go," wrote Zack, "and I can't say I'll be sorry to be home. It's been an experience, as they say, but the things I've learned are the strangest things, for instance, that I long to see you . . ."

Sarah, who had been playing Sinatra rather loudly, turned the tape recorder off and settled down to read the letter again, more quietly. After all, Frank had been singing "All or Nothing At All" and Sarah knew herself for a superstitious female.

On the following pages are details of Arrow books that will be of interest.

UNREPENTANT WOMEN

Judith Burnley

'A bold, brave, true and touching story' *Sunday Express*

Sarah Cornish is, in every way, a woman of her times. Intelligent, independent, attractive and worldly, Sarah has a family, a career and a life she loves.

At work, Sarah is planning a series of magazine articles about women whose stormy, controversial lives have been encouraging examples to all women. At home, however, Sarah is suddenly forced to face the other side of the coin in the person of her recently widowed mother-in-law. And Sarah — who has always seen herself as so bold and so free — comes to understand the secret fears and hidden strengths that lie at the centre of all women's lives.

Powerful, thought-provoking, witty and movingly honest, UNREPENTANT WOMEN is that rare creation — a novel that sees women the way they really are and not the way others would like them to be.

'Her observations twinkle; little escapes her. A serious book, funny too.' *Birmingham Post*

'Funny, sharp-eyed, sympathetic and moving. . .'
Philippa Toomey

Coming soon!

LOVE AND WORK

Gwyneth Cravens

When Angela Lee meets Joe Bly it is love at first sight. Not attraction, not curiosity, not lust, but Love. Love like the tide. Love like a ten-megaton bomb. But Joe Bly is more than the great passion of Angela's life – he is her boss as well.

Freud said that everyone needs love and work. But Freud wasn't young, female, beautiful – or in love with Joe.

'Perfect' *The New York Times*

'Delicious' *Daily Express*

'If Jane Austen lived in the Big Apple she might have written with the same pleasing mixture of compassion and wicked accuracy' *Punch*

Publication date: 28 July 1983

LOVE, MARY

Mary Gwynn

P.S. – This is a novel by Mary Gwynn

What is life really like for a single young woman on her own in a throbbing metropolis? Is it glamorous and sexy? Is every moment packed with romance and excitement and the possibility of adventure? Is it truly the only place to be if you are young, bright and eager to taste Life?

But what if you live in a 1½-room apartment with 500,000 cockroaches and no heat, in an expensive neighbourhood that is only reputed to be safe? What if your bank won't let you take out your own money because you accepted a Big Apple garden tool premium when you opened your account, your latest boyfriend has just left you for an older woman and your secretary has written a book entitled *Where's My Coffee, Boy? Memoirs of a Male Typist*?

What then?

Price to be confirmed

Fran Lebowitz
SOCIAL STUDIES

The American bestseller from the author of *Metropolitan Life*

With elegance and accuracy, Fran Lebowitz draws a knife through urban life, dissecting its pretensions, puncturing its sensitive joints and bursting more than one overblown bubble. Woody Allen may have his finger on the pulse of metropolitan society – but Fran Lebowitz has unblinkingly, unashamedly and unrepentantly cut out its heart.

'Should you make it through this book without laughing, have your vital signs checked – a deep coma is nothing to trifle with'
Cosmopolitan

'The funniest woman in America'
John Heilpern, *The Observer*

'You laugh out loud while wincing'   *Washington Post*

'Right on target'   *Punch*

£1.50

REPRISE

Claire Rayner

Maggy Dundas has everything. She is a brilliant jazz pianist with fame, style, looks and a sharp mind. She has the world at the end of her highly insured fingertips. But her happiness has always been marred by her painful memories and her bitter hatred for her mother. Now all that is over.

But Maggy's mother has left her one final bequest. It is a bequest that will irrevocably change Maggy's life and set her on an intricate, dangerous trail winding through time to the shady secrets of the past. Too late, Maggy discovers that nothing is over and that yesterday's fears and scandals have returned to haunt her.

£1.35